A Storybook ROMANCE

Love Unexpected
A Storybook ROMANCE

Three Romantic Novellas

MELANIE JACOBSON
JENNIFER K. CLARK • JULIE DAINES

Covenant Communications, Inc.

Cover Image: *Romantic Scene of Love* © Noppasin. Image courtesy of istockphoto.com

Published by Covenant Communications, Inc.
American Fork, Utah

Printed in the United States of America
First Printing: January 2015

21 20 19 18 17 16 15 10 9 8 7 6 5 4 3 2 1

ISBN: 978-1-62108-934-6

Storybook Romance

by

MELANIE JACOBSON

To the searchers
Keep looking. Love is out there.

Chapter 1

Ellie Hanover shouldn't have been one bit surprised to see Meredith Turin stripping their boss's office faster than Ed's body could cool in the morgue. But she *was* surprised. And it made her angry with herself that she had ever expected anything different.

She stared through the window into Ed's office, frowning as Meredith oversaw the removal of a framed print of the Erie Canal, the setting for the novel that had marked the first National Book Award for one of Ed's authors. Meredith had already banished all the other art, as well as the cigar humidor Ed had brought in for the first Pulitzer-winning project he'd edited. If he had loved a book all the way to his bones, there was some symbol for it on his shelves, desk, or walls.

Or there had been until an hour ago.

Meredith was dismantling all of it as if Ed's presence in her new space was an inconvenience and not as if his absence was the greatest tragedy in Ellie's professional life. Ellie sat down at her own desk, refusing to think about what it would mean to be in Meredith's direct line of sight now, and focused on the cream stationery in front of her. How did she even begin a note of condolence after a loss like this? Already, there was an Ed-sized hole in her life. How much worse was it for the family he'd so suddenly left behind?

She tried anyway. *Dear Helene, I'm so sorry. Ed was a great man . . .* She scribbled the rest of the note out and sighed after she signed her name. Everything she'd said was perfectly true and totally inadequate. Tomorrow her mentor would be buried, and she'd be more adrift than she'd been before he'd plucked her out of editorial obscurity and groomed her for the corner office Meredith was redecorating.

Ellie swiveled her chair, trying to block the view of Meredith's antics, but an explosion of glass drew her right back. One of the workmen had dropped a shadow box containing Ed's first edition of *The Adventures of Huckleberry Finn.* The fragile book now lay splayed on the carpeting next to Ellie's cubicle, its pages folded beneath it. She practically leaped over her partition to get to it. "Don't!" she called to the maintenance guy, who was about to snag it from the floor. She knelt and lifted it, holding her breath until the book was safely closed again.

A shadow fell over her as she examined the book, and Meredith's spicy sandalwood perfume wafted down to meet her. It made Ellie's nose twitch.

"What are you doing?" Meredith's cold voice scraped along Ellie's raw nerves.

She hated to crouch at Meredith's feet, but she couldn't leave the book undefended. "That guy dropped Ed's *Huck Finn.* I'm trying to assess the damage."

"Sorry," the workman said, sounding bored.

"You're making it difficult for the movers to get in and out of the office," Meredith said.

Ellie reined in a thousand objections that desperately wanted to fling themselves at Meredith. At best, they would bounce right off of her. More likely, they would irritate her into stinging back, and Meredith had suddenly gained the position in which her sting could devastate Ellie professionally.

So instead of shouting her accusations, Ellie took a deep breath. "Helene is going to want this. It's the least we can do for Ed."

Meredith summoned a plastic smile. "Of course we want to make sure this gets to Helene, but this is one of those instances I keep talking about where you can improve your efficiency."

It was almost enough to break the tight hold Ellie held on her temper, but she bit the inside of her cheek and forced her own return smile. "You're right," she said, standing and holding the book as gently as she could by its edges. "I'm just glad the book is okay."

"Yes, that's excellent." Meredith's eyebrows rose in expectation, and Ellie realized Meredith was waiting for her to move out of the way. She stepped back and bumped into the wall next to hers, sending a small avalanche of paper onto Tyler's desk, her neighbor in the cubicle farm.

"Sorry," she murmured.

"Totally okay," he answered back with a defiant glint in his eye. It surprised her. He was barely out of college, a rare hire out of their intern program, and his usual MO was to push his glasses up and duck behind his computer when trouble started.

Ellie hoped Meredith hadn't caught it. She was quick to put people on her hit list, and Tyler was too good of a guy and too new in his career to deserve that. The past year had sucked for Ellie ever since she'd earned her way into Meredith's crosshairs. Meredith had been a bad enemy before, but now? Ellie's brain hadn't yet wrapped around what it would mean to have her as her direct boss. She'd have to process it soon, but all she wanted at the moment was to figure out how to protect Ed's most favorite possessions for his kids. She owed him that, and even that small action helped her focus beyond her shock.

She slipped back to her own desk and set the book on top of her file cabinet, careful to put it somewhere it couldn't accidentally be bumped. She'd work out a way to get it to Helene right after she finished watching the maintenance crew dismantle Ed's office so she could write down every single thing they removed from it. She tensed for the next two hours, ready to spring into action to rescue any other treasures they manhandled, but they removed everything else without incident.

By the time the building began to empty of people, nothing tangible remained in Ed's space of the kind man who had believed in her before she'd had the faith to believe in herself.

She powered down her computer and packed her work bag, a Tiffany-blue leather satchel she'd treated herself to after signing her first writer for Hutton Publishing. She wrapped *Huck Finn* as snugly as she could in her thin spring coat and hugged it to her chest. She hoped it was enough to buffer it on her crowded subway ride home. It was the least she could do for the man who had given her everything.

Chapter 2

IT WAS BIZARRE TO WAKE up for the second day in a row to a world with no Ed. It wouldn't process that once again she'd have to drag herself into work and spend the better part of the day watching Meredith put her own relentlessly cutting-edge stamp on everything.

She'd earned it, Ellie supposed. Meredith had brought in new authors at a high volume, and they had sold well. Ultimately, that was what drove the profits that padded everyone's bonus checks. None of them were books Ellie would have taken on, but it was hard to argue with results. There was a huge audience for the fast-paced, sensational novels Meredith had a knack for ferreting out. But those books were Hershey's, and Ellie preferred Godiva. Selling more of something didn't make it better.

Ed had been trying to get Ellie to internalize the truth that success lay somewhere in the middle, that she needed to develop the eye that allowed her to spot not just a manuscript that moved her but one that would move *other people* enough to buy it at a rate that the author earned royalties. It was harder than it sounded. The strange reality of publishing was that 80 percent of the novels lost money for their publishers. Meredith specialized in the disposable-but-easy-to-digest projects that paid the bills. And that was how she'd scored the office Ed had left behind.

Job security wasn't the most important thing Ed had represented for Ellie. But it was near the top of the list. And that had evaporated overnight. Meredith didn't like her, and Ellie suspected that Meredith would be looking to get rid of her at the soonest possible moment.

Ellie's faint hope that she was worried about nothing crumpled like cheap paper the moment she arrived at work and found the maintenance guys back, this time packing *her* cubicle, winding cords with thoughtless efficiency and no consideration that they were sticking her entire professional life into three medium-sized boxes.

She sped past them straight to Meredith's office. Meredith peered at her over her glasses, which Ellie suspected were more of a fashion statement than a necessity.

"Do you know what's happening at my desk?"

Meredith glanced past her and then returned her attention to her computer screen. "It makes more sense for Amberly to sit there since she and I work together so closely. I'm moving Tyler too so Paige can have that spot."

Of course Meredith would want Paige, her assistant, close by. But moving Amberly was a slap—she and Ellie were both associate editors, so the only reason for the move was to signal Ellie's shift to the bottom of the pecking order.

It wasn't "You're fired," which is what Ellie had thought she'd hear, and relief flooded her, making her feel like a dog licking the boot that had kicked it. *Thanks for publicly humiliating me by moving my office without my knowledge. Just glad I still have a job.*

At least she hadn't made a show of questioning the workmen. No one needed to know that she hadn't seen this coming. She'd go out there and act relieved about the change.

In a way, she *was* relieved. She'd dreaded having to sit in front of Meredith's office for the bulk of her waking life. If Meredith wanted to move her two favorite lapdogs closer to her, Ellie almost saw an upside. She smiled at Meredith, smothering her own annoyance.

"I love that we're on the same wavelength."

One of Meredith's eyebrows flew up, but she straightened it again immediately. "Good. Then I'm sure what I'm going to say next will come as no surprise either. It's time to rethink your assignment here."

Now Ellie was getting fired? Why go through the pretense of moving her desk? Meredith smiled, and it sent a shiver through Ellie. She guessed that was probably how wolves looked right before they brought a deer down.

"Ed had so much faith in your taste and judgment," Meredith said. "It was remarkable."

"Thank you."

"I admit I haven't always seen it, but I figure he got where he did for a reason, and I should have a more open mind. We're really going to test those hidden talents of yours. I'm moving you to slush submissions. Let's see what gems you can mine from there."

Ellie swallowed. Six months ago she had eaten bad Chinese, so bad the stomach cramps had kept her home from work for a day. The same sick feeling seized her now. The slush pile was the bottomless inbox of unsolicited manuscripts sent in mainly by novice writers. Sometimes new agents who hadn't proven themselves with any breakout clients yet represented the authors, but far more often, no one at all represented them. They just typed up a four-hundred-page manuscript and sent it out with no concept of how publishing worked and, worse, with no concept of how to tell a good story.

Even if Meredith didn't change Ellie's title or pay, it would be the same as if she had done both once word spread around the office. Ellie would lose any chance of finding sellable books, which meant no chance for bonuses. She'd earn the pity and scorn of the entire Hutton staff, and before long, it would be hard to justify her professional existence. Then Meredith could fire her without any backlash.

Ellie summoned her bravest face and hoped she looked unperturbed. "That sounds great. I guess Ed must have mentioned how much I like working with new talent." *Ha. There's not an ounce of talent in the eight hundred e-mails currently waiting for a purging. I'm so dead.* "I'm going to make sure these guys get my stuff over there in one piece."

Meredith didn't acknowledge Ellie's exit, her eyes already back on her monitor.

When Ellie passed Tyler, he gave her a sympathetic smile. For being at least five years younger than she was and far newer to Hutton, he'd gotten a feel for the politics pretty quickly. She threw back a smile that showed she was fine with this change, a careless tilt of the lips intended to hide the fear pushing up from the pit in her stomach.

Her days were numbered at Hutton, and she'd have to scramble like crazy to figure something out. She followed the workmen down to her new desk and fought a frustrated groan when she saw how close it was to reception. The closer to the lobby, the lower you ranked.

While she oversaw the workmen reconnecting the jumble of cords to the various devices on her new desk, she returned the smiles of her new cubicle mates. She tried to look happy with the change while she struggled to solve the massive problem her job had just become, but answers slipped away from her, scattering like pigeons before a toddler in Central Park.

When the workmen left, she sat down and pulled out the only framed photo she kept on her desk. It was of her dressed in her graduation cap and gown, standing with a tiny Latina woman named Brenda Martinez. Brenda had been the first person to ever see Ellie as more than a case file.

Brenda had done a tremendous amount of shoving, but her stubbornness had landed Ellie in college, where she had thrived in classes she'd never dreamed were options, where she had soaked up literature and composition courses and reveled in the richness of language as she had never before experienced it. She'd excelled enough to earn scholarships for her last two years and land herself a TA position at NYU while she worked on a master's in literature.

That had led to her internship at Hutton, where she'd come to Ed's attention after disagreeing with him when he asked her to draft a rejection notice for a manuscript. The rest was history.

And she was about to become history again if she didn't do something to change the one-way ticket out that Meredith had punched for her. She forced herself to access the e-mail folder every associate editor dreaded facing. Meredith had basically just ordered her to hunt for the needle in this wordstack—blindfolded—but it was the only option Ellie had at the moment. Brenda had taught her to take advantage of even the tiniest opportunities, so with a deep breath and a prayer for the best luck of her life, she opened the slush folder.

* * *

A week had passed. A week in which the pitying glances had begun to fade and people in the Hutton fiction division had divided themselves into two camps: those who had been stepped on by Meredith at some point, and those who hadn't and would avoid it at any cost. The former were Ellie's allies, she quickly discovered. Often, they offered help in subtle ways, hints about how to make Amberly's and Paige's jobs harder without drawing attention to herself. They loaned supplies and helped her navigate glitchy computer issues. Their lips tightened or their eyes went blank when Meredith's name came up.

The other group kept their distance to avoid the taint of associating with Meredith's most recent casualty.

Ellie tried to ignore it all. She'd been going through dozens of manuscripts a day, sending a form rejection letter on most of them after only twenty pages. They all sounded either alike or so far out there that they were unintelligible. The ones that at least made sense read like they had been constructed from a storytelling kit. All the parts were there, but every single one of them lacked a spark.

It was sucking the life right out of her. To make it worse, Amberly had just that morning kicked down a copyediting job that should have gone to a junior staffer. It was an insult, but Ellie had bitten back her frustration and smiled, promising to return it to her soon.

Instead of clicking on the next submission in her inbox, Ellie opened a new browser window. It would take only a few keystrokes to call up a job-search website . . . but her hands hovered above the keyboard. Publishing was a volatile industry, and jobs within in it were harder to get than a taxi in rush hour. If she quit Hutton, she'd be changing her career, not just her job.

Her inner nine-year-old self rebelled at the thought. Before Brenda had saved Ellie, books had. She'd lost herself for hours, even days, in reading after she'd discovered *Anne of Green Gables*, another orphan's story unfolding a hundred years ago on Prince Edward Island. The Anne series had been her only companion during the last half of elementary school and the one quiet place inside the chaos of her life.

Ellie wanted to be a part of making that kind of magic, of finding the beautiful manuscripts and plucking them out of the piles shuffled to her by hungry agents. She wanted to polish them until they shone and give them to the world. She hated the idea that the cheap and easy books Meredith cranked out might swallow up the beautiful things. Her nine-year-old self, the Ellie who had loved books more than anyone had ever loved anything, demanded that she try.

She closed the browser. Three more weeks. She'd give herself twenty-one more days to find *the* story, the one that would breathe something good back into the thin air of Hutton, that would make it all right again.

Chapter 3

As it turned out, she needed sixteen days to reach a manuscript called *Walking Home.* It had an agent, Darren Lansing, whose name she didn't recognize. Red flag. But the cover letter he had included on behalf of his client intrigued her.

The story was set in an Afghan village outside of Kabul. The agent described a story about the unbreakable ties between a mother and child, a story of hardship and hope. But the author was male, someone named Max Crowe. Another red flag. She loved the idea of the story, but a man telling a mother/daughter relationship in a real way? No.

Something about his name niggled at her until she got to his credentials—foreign correspondent for the *Metro Times*? Of course. She'd read a series he'd done last year about an Afghan man called the Shepherd, only his flock was the maimed and homeless children displaced by war and the Taliban. Her fingers fumbled in her rush to open the manuscript.

"The rain fell without regard for the people beneath it, not those who cheered its coming or those who cursed its arrival. It came anyway and blanketed everything, giving and taking with every drop." Two sentences, and Ellie fell into the story. By page three, she'd lost all doubt about Max Crowe's ability to tell this story. By page twenty, she was convinced he'd been born to write it.

She didn't look up until Tyler tapped on her cubicle wall to invite her to lunch, and she only waved him away with an apology. He gave her a small, knowing smile; they all lived for the days where they found the stories they wanted more than food.

Ellie read for four hours, ignoring her e-mails and phone calls. It wasn't until Amberly came down the hallway in a snit that Ellie looked up from the screen that held the world Max Crowe had opened to her.

"Why aren't you answering your phone?" Amberly demanded.

Ellie blinked at the red light on her voice mail. "I didn't hear it ring. Sorry."

"It's sitting two feet away from you," Amberly said, her voice even tighter.

"I really am sorry," Ellie said. "What can I do for you?"

"The copyedits that were due two hours ago."

"Sorry. I finished those this morning." Ellie tapped on the keyboard for a few brief moments and smiled up at Amberly again. "There. I sent them to you. Sorry again about the delay."

Amberly's eyes narrowed. "What has you so distracted anyway?" she asked, craning to look at Ellie's screen.

Ellie smiled and minimized the window showing the manuscript. "It's nothing," she said. "Just a project that looked interesting. Won't go anywhere, I'm sure." That was a lie. It was far too rich and quiet for Meredith's taste, but Ellie was determined to make it go somewhere despite that. Looking at Amberly, she felt the same tickle of unease that plagued her whenever the subway train ran late on a hot summer evening and she was stuck breathing the fumes of too many people in a tight space. Worse than the smell was the energy a crowd like that had, a restlessness that always seemed one wrong move away from degenerating into pushing and shoving and ugliness. Ellie felt that now, so she kept her smile fixed, not willing to let Amberly know exactly how riveted she'd been to the manuscript.

Amberly stayed put for a moment, waiting for Ellie to do or say something that would give her a hint that there was more going on, but Ellie didn't waver. She already loved the manuscript too much to risk a slipup. Amberly had seen Ellie as her biggest competition for promotion once she'd realized she'd made a tactical error in sucking up to Meredith instead of Ed. She'd won, really, but Ellie suspected Amberly was more interested in total annihilation.

Amberly tucked a dark strand of hair behind her ear and frowned. "You should have sent these proofs over as soon as they were done. You're going to have to get faster, because I have a lot more for you to do."

Ellie opened her mouth to protest that she was faster than anyone else Amberly had and it wasn't even her job, but she snapped it shut again. No use challenging her. She'd only make Ellie's job harder, and it was already close to impossible since Meredith put her on slush duty. A hint of satisfaction flashed in Amberly's eyes, and she turned without a word to march back to her own desk on heels way too high for a ten-hour workday.

As soon as Amberly was out of sight, Ellie's fingers flew, calling up the e-mail from Darren Lansing, desperate to settle a new fear that had risen now that she was outside the spell of Max Crowe's story: how long ago had this manuscript been sent? Because anyone with a functioning heart and half a brain would have snapped it up already if they'd read it.

She checked the date on his original message. It had been almost six weeks ago. If *Walking Home* had gone to the slush pile of all the other major publishing houses, there was a small chance it was still available, and she fanned that hope to brightness because she wanted it to be true. She *needed* the book. It made her numb insides feel as if they'd been pushed to their limits and filled with the possibility of good in the world. And maybe more importantly, this was *the* book, the one she'd been dying to find for months, even before Meredith had taken over Ed's job.

Hoping against hope, she typed out an e-mail to the agent and sent it off with a prayer that for the first time since Ed died, things would take a turn for the good.

Chapter 4

DEAR MS. HANOVER,

We're pleased that you enjoyed Walking Home. *It's a tremendous book, quiet but powerful, and it's exciting that you recognize that. The manuscript, while out with other publishers, is still available. We would be interested in hearing your vision for the book.*

Kind regards,

Darren Lansing

Ellie barely refrained from a fist pump. Then she wondered why she was refraining and fist pumped anyway. The first obstacle was out of the way; the novel wasn't under contract anywhere, and that meant she could bring it to the editorial board. Right?

She could still do that, couldn't she? Normally the board, made up of the executive editor down to the associates like herself, met every two weeks to discuss which projects they wanted to acquire. It was a competitive meeting because Hutton took on a limited number of projects a year, and everyone was pushing their manuscripts. If the board decided it was a good gamble, the acquiring editor would make an offer to the author, and the long process of getting their book on the market began.

For most editors, if the book did well, they saw the payoff of the sales in their bonus checks. So far, three of the books Ellie had championed had made it to market. The bonuses didn't amount to much because, even though all three books had been very well-reviewed, they saw only modest sales. The low sales would work against her when pitching this book to the board, but the positive reviews would work in her favor. The higher-ups at Hutton loved the cash flow that Meredith's projects transfused into the company coffers, but they liked the prestige of the reviews. At some point, she'd find a book that offered both, and that's when she'd climb to the next tier on the company ladder.

That was all assuming she had a chance to argue for *Walking Home*. The last board meeting was two weeks ago, and Paige had e-mailed that Meredith would prefer for Ellie to work on a proofreading deadline instead of attending. It stung that Meredith hadn't even told her herself, but it hadn't been an outright "You will no longer be needed here" directive. So maybe the door to the conference room was still open . . .

She sighed and sent the agent query and first three chapters of *Walking Home* to print. She would have to face Meredith to find out if she had a shot of presenting this brilliant story to the board in two days.

* * *

Thursday morning, Ellie marched straight to Meredith's office before she could lose the courage she'd been screwing up on the subway ride from home. She blew past Amberly, who glared at her, and Paige, who called after her when she knocked and stepped into Meredith's office without waiting for an invitation.

Once again, Ellie experienced a pang as the sheer lack of Ed-ness in the room washed over her. The garish paperback covers of Meredith's most successful projects lined the wall, each looking a lot like the next. She glanced away, not wanting the sameness of them to depress her.

Meredith eyed her, annoyance written in the straight slash of her mouth. "You're not on my schedule."

"I know," Ellie said, pushing aside the thought that no one had ever needed a schedule to see Ed. Comparisons wouldn't help. "It's just that I know the editorial board meets today, and I wondered if you'd had a chance to look over *Walking Home.* I think it would be wond—"

"Look over what?" Meredith said, her attention now on the notebook in front of her.

"The novel I dropped by on Tuesday? I gave you the first three chapters?" Ellie hated that Meredith's lack of interest had undermined her so quickly that suddenly all of her sentences were coming out as questions. She swallowed and tried again. "It came out of the slush, and I'm shocked. I think it's because it's repped by a new agent, but I'm pretty sure if we don't grab this book, Waltman or Beacher will jump on it as soon as they realize they have it too." She named their biggest competitors, and Meredith glanced up.

"It's a bad investment," she said.

"So you read it?" Ellie asked.

"I glanced at it. It's not what we're looking for right now," Meredith said, waving her hand as if she were sweeping the manuscript away.

"But I think if you read the whole thing, you'd find it mind-blowing. I already thought about how to present this to the board, and—"

Meredith laughed. "That wasn't a great way to spend your time, Ellie. What do you think you're going to tell them that would make them take on a loser like this one? It won't even earn out its advance, much less get a reprinting."

There had to be a way to save this. There still had to be a place at Hutton for beautiful, challenging works that made the soul bigger. Because if there truly wasn't, that meant there wasn't a place for Ellie at Hutton, and she wasn't ready yet to give up that dream.

"Well?" Meredith snapped.

Ellie realized Meredith's question hadn't been rhetorical. She was expecting an answer about what Ellie would say to the board. "There's always room in the market for genius." It was one of Ed's favorite sayings, and Meredith's narrowed eyes told Ellie that she had heard Ed say it too. "This is the book people are going to give their friends and daughters and mothers. And not just this year but every year. It's a classic waiting to happen, and if we can give it a slow build, it'll pay out for us forever."

Meredith lifted her eyebrows. "That's it? That's your argument?"

Ellie nodded. It was absolutely the best one she could make because it was true.

"You'd better go back to the slush pile, Ellie. Though I'm beginning to wonder if you don't have the right eye for something like that."

Ellie fought a flinch and kept her voice steady. "I do, Meredith. I'm sorry you don't see it in this book, but I'll bring you another one."

Meredith's eyes were already back on her notebook when she muttered an absentminded, "Good luck with that."

Back at her desk, Ellie slumped into her seat and stared at the e-mail she'd composed earlier that sat ready to send when she won over the board this afternoon. It was informing Max Crowe's agent that they wanted to make an offer on the book. She could picture Crowe's face when his agent told him the news . . .

Wait. No, she couldn't. She'd invented a middle-aged, weather-beaten newspaper reporter who looked even older than his years because of the weight of experience in his face. But she had no idea what Crowe looked like. She hadn't even thought to look him up yet because she'd been so absorbed in his novel, but she suddenly couldn't resist investigating further who this person was whose story had wrung her heart out and then pieced it back together. She typed his name into Google, knowing it was only another way to avoid writing the rejection she had to send. The search returned a link to Crowe's blog.

She clicked on his "About the Author," and a picture popped up. Her breath caught. This was no grizzled war correspondent. He was barely thirty, if that. The smile lines around his eyes and the gold streaks running through his light-brown hair suggested he'd spent a fair amount of time in the sun, but there was no cynicism carved into the lines of his face like she'd expect for someone who had spent several years reporting from war-torn countries. She clicked on the thumbnail photo, anxious to see more details. The bigger picture showed dark blue eyes, and despite the easy smile he wore, there was something sad about them in close up.

She closed the window before anyone could wonder why she was magnifying photos of hot guys on her work computer. Instead, she clicked back to his blog posts and read. An hour later, she was half in love with him. He had a touch with language that she'd rarely seen. While his blog posts weren't as lyrical as his manuscript had been, they burst with emotion that his *Metro Times* articles had only hinted at.

Tyler brought her back to reality when he wandered over to borrow a pair of scissors, and once she obliged him, she turned back to the screen with her heart even heavier.

This was what she had to reject. She hadn't been overstating the case when she'd described his writing as genius. His blog posts confirmed it. Some of them had challenged her to think about her own lens for viewing the world. Others had reached inside her and twisted her guts as she'd read about lives unimaginably harder than her own. Or at least they *had* been unimaginable; Max Crowe had made it all too real with his ability to jerk the reader inside his descriptions and force them to walk around and see, really see, what was going on halfway across the world. And not just see but care.

Steeling herself to send the rejection she knew would haunt her for the rest of her career, she copied and pasted the standard "No, thank you" e-mail she usually sent. *Thanks for your interest in Hutton . . . not the right project . . . didn't connect with your characters.*

That one pulled her up short because it was a blatant lie. In the hours she'd spent reading the book, she'd more than connected with Crowe's characters. They'd become her friends, and she'd become their cheerleader as she'd yearned for their reunion, at times finding herself physically straining toward her computer as if she could somehow urge them toward each other, through danger, and back to home.

She deleted the form rejection and started over.

Dear Mr. Lansing:

I've never been so sorry to send a rejection letter as I am right now. Walking Home *was one of the most beautiful pieces I've read in all my time here at Hutton, and that's why it pains me to inform you that we have to pass. The market isn't quite right for something like this, and with the world of publishing still reeling from all the changes it has experienced over the last five years, now is the wrong time for us to take a risk.*

Speaking personally, there's no risk I wouldn't take for the privilege of being the editor to help this novel find its way into the world. But I've been overruled, and so stepping back into my professional capacity,

I'm unable to offer Hutton as the new home for the literary genius of Mr. Crowe. I sincerely hope his work finds the home it richly deserves.
Kindest regards,
Ellie Hanover

She pressed send, and it was as if the action drew the last bit of hope out of her with the click of the mouse. As soon as she got home, she'd start submitting her résumé to some of the job sites she'd seen advertised on the sides of city buses and on the Times Square billboards. There was no point in waiting out the full three weeks. This was never going to work, and she couldn't lie to herself about that anymore.

When the résumés were submitted, she'd console herself with a pint of ice cream, a giant spoon, and the sweet torture of reading through the blog archives of one Mr. Crowe.

* * *

Ellie pressed the heels of her hands into her eyes to keep any tears from slipping out, but it was too late. They were falling and wouldn't go back in. She gave up and blinked through them to finish the blog post that had sparked them. She'd been reading Max Crowe's blog since she got home, picking up where she'd left off at work. All of these so far had been filed from Afghanistan. The word pictures he painted ranged from hilarious to heartbreaking, and he drew landscapes she'd never imagined and painted portraits of people she felt she was coming to know within the space of a column.

But this last piece was the clear root of *Walking Home.* He'd written about going on a routine patrol with an army squad assigned to walk through one of the villages outside of Kabul, scouting for trouble or offering any help that might be needed. At the village center, they'd seen a young girl of about eleven, filthy with road dirt, limping as if she'd been walking for a thousand miles already. A woman squatting in front of one of the huts caught Max Crowe's eye because she held herself in a way that suggested she was waiting, but she'd been that way for over two hours already. Suddenly the woman spotted the girl and flowed up to her feet; a cry tore from her throat as she broke into a run. The girl froze and then collapsed as soon as the woman reached her, falling into the woman's arms as if her body had only held enough steps in it to get her to this woman and no farther. They wept. And Ellie did too.

But now, dashing the tears away, she felt a sense of guilt because she'd taken in so much from Max Crowe's stories and given nothing back. It would be weird and stalkerish for her to comment on something written two years before . . . but she needed to. She had to let him know the words mattered. She clicked in the comment box and thought for a moment about what to say.

This piece is a gift to anyone who has ever lost someone. I feel like I lived for a moment in that little girl's shoes as she found her someone again. It's not actually possible for me, but for a few minutes, I imagined what it would be like to be reunited with my lost one. I haven't thought about that in years, and it made everything better for a few minutes. So thank you.

She hesitated over the field that asked for her name. She didn't want to put Ellie because if he hadn't seen her rejection on behalf of Hutton yet, he would soon. She typed her full name instead: Eleanor. Then she clicked to post it and put her laptop away. She'd mined deep enough into her emotions for one evening.

She busied herself with her nighttime routine and climbed into bed. For the first time in a long time, she dreamed about her mom and woke up feeling equal parts happy and sad.

The next morning, she stumbled to the kitchen for her coffee and sat down to check her e-mail. Maybe she'd gotten a nibble on her résumé. She'd be able to better face another day at Hutton if she had an exit plan. When her inbox opened, her breath hitched like it had the one time she'd talked herself into going to the top of the Empire State building. There were no messages from job recruiters, but Max Crowe had replied to her blog comment. Her fingers tangled in her rush to click his message open.

I guess we're even because this comment was a gift to me tonight. It reminded me that maybe there's a reason I was given the impulse to write. At least once a day I think that there has to be a smarter way for me to earn a living, but nothing else ever feels right. All this rambling is to say that I appreciate you taking the time to comment. It came at exactly the right moment.

Like all of his blog posts, he'd said so much in the space of a few sentences. She had a sinking feeling that his tone of self-doubt was a result of her rejection letter. But at the same time, her cheeks warmed to think of him reading her comment and feeling like it mattered.

Did he really not understand how powerful his writing was? She glanced at the clock. If she went with a bun instead of trying to straighten her hair, she'd have enough time to leave another comment before work. She clicked through Max's blog archives and wondered when she'd come to think of him as Max, not Max Crowe. When he'd written back, she decided. When he'd become more than a byline.

She found the post she was looking for, a piece about a boy who was supporting his younger brother and sister by selling goat's milk to people who had barely more than he did. Twin themes of despair and hope ran through the story, something she'd come to recognize as a signature of Max's work. It didn't seem possible that this boy could make it, yet something in the way Max described the set of the boy's shoulders, the look in his streetwise eyes, made her think the underage milk merchant had a chance. A few times, Max had posted follow-up stories about people he had profiled, where-are-they-now updates, but Ellie hadn't seen anything for the enterprising boy, and she wanted one.

Since Max's response to her had come from his e-mail address, she replied directly back to it.

To: Max Crowe
From: Eleanor H
RE: Blog Comment

I'm glad my comment encouraged you, but truly, your work is . . . incredible.

Ellie squirmed as she looked at the words on the screen, but she let them stand. They were the truth, and if she couldn't tell the truth to someone stationed a world away in Afghanistan, who could she tell? She thought about him in the war-gutted country as foreign to her as Mars. Someone who sacrificed easy living to report on reality deserved reality in return. She forged ahead before her nerves could get the better of her.

After each of your blog posts I read, I'm sitting here wondering so many things. They're the big questions, the ones no one can answer. How did it get so bad there? How does goodness still exist in spite of all that? And how can anyone fix it?

That felt so heavy, so she tried for a joke.

You're clear eyed. Maybe you know. You should take a stab at it. How can we solve Afghanistan? I'll wait, but I have to go to work soon, so we'll need to figure this out quickly, and by "we" I mean YOU . . . (Imagine me tapping my watch impatiently.)

There. That should give the whole thing the right tone. She hit send and hurried into her tiny bedroom to wrangle her hair into a cooperative knot at her nape. She slipped on a black dress—one of many, many practical black dresses she owned—and flats. She checked her reflection and winced. She looked like the headmistress of a Russian ballet academy, but there wasn't time to do more. She paused at her kitchen table to shut her laptop. Max had already replied.

To: Eleanor H
From: Max Crowe
RE: Blog post

You don't ask for much, do you? Solve Afghanistan, huh? Why didn't I think of that? Here's my first plan: you stand outside of the prime minister's office and do that watch-tapping thing. It should intimidate him into pulling the country together. I can almost smell the Nobel Peace Prize in my future for thinking of it. I'll mention you in my speech.

She laughed. How could she not? Nothing about the situation was funny, but he had the same gallows humor she'd used her whole life. It had pulled her through every one of the wretched years she'd spent in foster care. Laugh, or it would kill her. She heard the echoes of the same kind of laughter in his jokes.

To: Max Crowe
From: Eleanor H
RE: Blog Comment

What exactly does a Nobel Peace Prize smell like?

She sent the reply and had her hand on the door when her IM alert sounded. The table shook when she skidded into it in her rush to see if it was Max. It was.

She had maybe five minutes' leeway before she would be irreparably late for work, but as Meredith's cold face flashed through her head, she sat down and accepted the request.

MC: Musky with a slight note of citrus.
EH: Sounds refreshing.
MC: It'll wake you up better than coffee.
*EH: Better than coffee? *Shakes head.* In case you were wondering, that's where your lie fell apart. Nothing is better than coffee.*
MC: You found me out.
EH: I can't consort with tale tellers. I'm off.
MC: Hold up. What if I told really good tales?
EH: Well . . . you kind of already do.
MC: Thank you.
EH: Sure. Gotta run to work.
MC: Oh, right. Forgot the time.

Of course he had. Ellie tapped out a good-bye and made a mental note to look at a world clock to find out exactly what time it was in Afghanistan.

It ended up being the only interesting thing she did that day. Paige e-mailed her a proofreading assignment, which was a new low. Now Meredith was delegating her assistant—not even Amberly—to assign Ellie menial tasks? Ellie plowed through it but stopped an hour before lunch to take an aspirin when she realized she'd been clenching her jaw so tightly all morning that it ached. During lunch, she nearly flew out of the office, desperate for a space between herself and the walls of her cubicle.

She sat on a bench across the street from the Hutton building and scrolled through her e-mails on her phone. There was nothing from Max. It bummed her out, and she snorted at her own absurdity. He didn't know anything about her—not her real name or her age or how she looked. They'd traded a few jokes because she'd been stalkerish enough to read through his years-old blog archives and he'd been kind enough to respond. And maybe he did appreciate a little communication out there in the battle zone. She couldn't fault him for that. But it was silly to pretend they had connected at the kindred-spirit level, as Anne Shirley would have said. It had been a couple of e-mails and an IM chat, and that was it.

She went back to her e-mails: a notice from the public library that she had something due . . . an offer from her favorite off-Broadway theater . . . and a request for a job interview.

She tapped it open. A travel magazine was looking for an editor. She frowned. A month ago, she wouldn't have dreamed of switching to magazine work. But now, staring up at Hutton, she couldn't imagine staying there any longer. She didn't want to trade the depth and complexity of novels for the quick pace of a monthly journal, but Ellie was tired of the constant Meredith chill in the office.

She hit reply to *Tasteful Travel's* inquiry. Yes, she would be pleased to come in for an interview the following week. She offered a time that corresponded with her lunch break, and with every syllable she typed, she became even more frustrated with Meredith for forcing her into accepting the interview.

She sent the message and sat back to glare up at the window to Meredith's office, half hoping her boss saw her. But she'd just be an indistinct smudge of black on the sidewalk from Meredith's vantage point.

There wasn't a more appropriate metaphor for her whole existence at Hutton since Ed's death.

Chapter 5

MC: You there?

Ellie blinked at the cursor on her laptop. It blinked back.

She shouldn't answer. Meredith had upped her drive-Ellie-to-quit pressure with a new tactic: giving her more work than she could do in a day. Ellie was no stranger to bringing work home with her, but the difference between working on a manuscript she had championed and slaving over proofreads on a trashy romance was like the difference between summering on a beach in the Hamptons and diving into a motel swimming pool.

But she had to finish. She wouldn't give Meredith the satisfaction of firing her before she could quit. And that meant she shouldn't distract herself with another long conversation with Max like she'd had the last three nights.

No, she definitely shouldn't. But she did.

EH: I'm here.

MC: I don't know where "there" is. How do I find out in a non-stalkery way?

EH: I'm nowhere interesting, I promise.

MC: Yeah, but my writerly imagination needs the details, or else I fill them in myself, and I'm neurotic enough to be bothered that I don't know if they're right.

EH: Go ahead. It's better than the boring truth.

MC: I think you hang out where there are a lot of intellectual heavyweights.

Well, that *used* to be true, in the Ed days.

EH: Maybe. Go on.
MC: A university somewhere. I'll bet you're a professor.
EH: Wrong.
MC: Give me a hint. The kind I can't use to track you down in case I'm a secret Hannibal Lecter.
EH: Ew.
MC: Bad comparison. I just mean that I'm tired of a blank in my head every time I imagine what your side of these conversations looks like. And since my imagination never listens to me, you should probably just put it to rest with a few details that don't reveal your actual secret location.

There was no way she could tell him what she did for a living. He'd figure out her connection to Hutton right away, and she didn't want him to know that she was the one who'd rejected his book. But she didn't want to be one of the lame people littering the Internet who lied about themselves either. She thought so long about what to say that he nudged her.

MC: Eleanor? If it makes you feel better, I have friends all over the world because of my column, and I've never stalked one of them.

Ellie considered that. What kind of friends? Max had come off bright and well-adjusted in their previous evening chats, but maybe that was an act?

EH: Why friends in so many places?
MC: Otherness. It fascinates me.
EH: Explain . . . ?
MC: I guess that's how I ended up in Afghanistan. People intrigue me, and the less like me they are, the more interested I am in figuring out what makes them tick. Somehow, it always turns out we're more the same than I expect.
EH: Otherness bothers me. I don't like being other.
MC: Don't you think it's what makes you intriguing?
EH: But I'm not! I feel bad for tricking you into thinking I am.
MC: You didn't trick me. I can just tell. Here's the thing . . .

A long pause followed—so long Ellie checked to make sure her Internet connection was still working. Finally, he typed.

MC: People often contact me through my blog to yell or tell me I'm wrong. And a lot even say thanks for writing a piece, like you did. And I always respond to the nice ones with a thank you. And every now and then a . . . correspondence happens. And that's how I make friends all over the world. I chat with Allah Abdoun. He's a tour guide in Egypt. And Blanche in London. She's a grandmother with a very British sense of humor. And there's Xochi, a dye-maker in Mexico, and Burl, a Canadian maple farmer. And you, in . . . ?

EH: Big City, USA.

MC: Ah, Big City. I know it well. And you do . . . ?

EH: I fix things.

It was true enough. She fixed manuscripts, stories, words.

MC: Tractor-sized things? Microchip-sized things? Building-size things?

EH: Things that are smaller than a pizza box and bigger than a matchbook.

MC: Hm. I've got it. You repair DVD players in the crowded back room of a family-run electronics store in Philadelphia.

EH: I'm insulted. You think I only got this job because my family runs the store? I'm GOOD.

MC: I believe it. Thank you, btw. I feel much better now that I can place you.

Ellie wanted to ask him where he was, whether he had to camp in a tent or sleep in a barrack or if journalists got nicer accommodations. But she suspected he sought out friends all over the world so he could escape his reality for a bit, and it didn't seem fair to ask him questions she wasn't willing to answer herself.

EH: No problem. I should go now. I have to fix something.

MC: A DVD player?

EH: A sandwich.

MC: Have you ever noticed that sandwiches always taste better when other people make them?

EH: I totally have! I thought I was the only one who thought that.

MC: Nope. It's a universal truth. Except when the mess hall cook at Bagram Airfield does it. I don't know how you screw up a sandwich, but he does.

EH: That's a tragedy.

MC: War. It even ruins sandwiches.

That startled a laugh out of her.

EH: Even so, I'm going to try to make my best sandwich and curl up with a book.

*MC: *Grunts.* Me no like books. Book smash.*

EH: Uh . . . what?

MC: Don't mind me. I'm throwing a temper tantrum because books and I have had a hard road this week.

That admission sent two different sensations through Ellie simultaneously. Her stomach dropped like an empty elevator with the guilt of not being able to get Max's book to the editorial board. And at the same time, anger tightened her jaw. *Walking Home* deserved to be read, and if Meredith couldn't see that, Ellie knew who could. She'd be leaving Hutton as soon as she sewed up another job, and after adding two more job interviews to her calendar next week, she didn't doubt that would be soon. She didn't owe the company any more loyalty. The thought squeezed her heart but hardened her resolve. Max's book wasn't dead yet. She had a contact somewhere else who would be very, very interested. She hoped.

EH: Sorry about your book issues. I have to run now.

MC: Catch you later, Big City Girl.

EH: Wait. How do you know I'm a girl? Maybe I'm a grandmother too.

MC: I do words for a living, remember? You don't "talk" like a grandmother. You sound young. But super smart! Wait, I don't mean "young" like immature. I mean it like . . .

A pause followed while the "Max Crowe is typing" prompt appeared and reappeared in the open chat window a couple of times.

He had to be typing and deleting while he tried to dig himself out of his word hole. Ellie considered helping him for a minute but then decided it would be more fun to see what he came up with.

MC: I meant youthful. Not like a grandmother. That's all.
EH: Good guess.
MC: Am I right?
*EH: *Shrugs.**
MC: It doesn't matter, you know. I just like knowing if my powers of observation are on point.
EH: Then I'm under thirty but well out of college. Good night, Mr. Crowe.
MC: Good night, Eleanor.

As soon as she logged off of their chat, she opened her e-mail to make right what Meredith had gotten so wrong. The strangeness of contacting her biggest competitor at Beacher Publishing fit her like too-small shoes, but Max deserved it. No, the world deserved it, because Ellie shouldn't be the only one who got to read his book. She composed the note to Andrew Bale, her counterpart at Beacher before Meredith's stupid political maneuvering had bumped her back to peon duty. Andrew had acquired some projects Ellie respected, and she had a feeling he'd need only a light nudge to see the merit in Max's novel. She sent it with a smile, knowing she'd done Max one of the biggest favors of his life, even though he'd never know it was her.

Chapter 6

"YOU'RE LATE," PAIGE SAID WHEN Ellie passed her desk the following Tuesday afternoon.

Paige's slightly nasally voice was always irritating. It was more irritating when Paige was commenting on things that were none of her business, but it was most irritating when she was right. Ellie's interview had gone wrong in every conceivable way, including starting a half hour late and putting her well over her scheduled lunchtime. Ellie gritted her teeth. Paige took so many coffee breaks during the day, *every* day, that her java runs easily doubled the length of Ellie's tardiness, but Ellie didn't point out the double standard, and she wasn't going to apologize for her lateness to Paige, of all people, either.

Instead, she kept walking without a word down the short stretch of carpet to her own desk, where she collapsed and dropped her head into her hands. Lucy, her cubicle neighbor, popped her head over their shared wall. "How did it go?" she asked, keeping her voice low. Lucy had actually been the one to tip her off to this interview. "You're too good for this," she'd whispered one day with a nod to the proofreading assignment on Ellie's screen. Then she'd slid over the job posting for an editing slot at an interior-design magazine.

Ellie hated to confess she'd bombed it. But she'd been out of place the second she'd set foot in their airy offices wearing her severe black dress while people in summer-weight clothes and bright colors had laughed and chatted at their desks. The wardrobe misstep, plus her total ignorance about designing interiors, had rattled her so badly that she'd stumbled on the executive editor's first question and bumbled her way through every one after that until he'd put her out of her misery by ending the interview.

"I don't think I got it," she said.

Lucy frowned. "They're idiots."

"No, it wasn't them. I . . . it was the wrong fit."

Lucy's expression left no doubt that she didn't think that was possible, but she let it go. "I'll keep an eye out for any other juicy-looking jobs. Let me know if there's anything I can do to help."

"Thanks."

Lucy moved as if to sit back down on her side.

"Wait," Ellie said. She cleared her throat. "I appreciate the help, but I'm sort of wondering . . . why? Why are you doing it?"

Lucy smiled. "I'm not going to lie. I can't stand Paige. Even though she's moved all the way down by Meredith's office, it's not far enough. So if I can get you something better than the job she and Amberly stole from you in the first place, then as far as I'm concerned, that's just good fun." Her eyes softened and turned down toward her hands. "Also, um . . ." She swallowed. "I'm not from here. I'm from Nebraska. And people there are a lot nicer than they are in New York. And you're one of the first people to really help me since I've been here, so thanks. Let's call this payback. The good kind."

Ellie blushed at the thanks. She'd spent an entire afternoon helping Lucy master their typesetting program. It had put her behind on one of Amberly's proofreading assignments, which had brought the pinch-mouthed brunette down to yell at her, but Ellie wasn't sorry. It had taken her forever to learn the program, and she didn't regret teaching Lucy some shortcuts despite Amberly's lecture on how being professional meant meeting deadlines. "It's what anyone would have done."

"No, it's not. Believe me, I've been at Hutton for more than a year, and it's not the norm. You're too nice to work here."

"Thanks. But Hutton's not really the problem. This place was pretty cool not that long ago."

"Under Ed," Lucy said.

"Under Ed," Ellie repeated, nodding.

"Well, I'm still going to help you get out."

Ellie felt heat creep up her cheeks again as she tried to figure out how to word her next question. "I could use a little help, actually. Would you . . . ?"

Lucy tilted her head. "Sure."

Ellie grinned. "You don't know what I was going to say."

"Yes, anyway. What is it?"

Ellie looked down at the boring black dress that mirrored a dozen others in her closet. "I think maybe I've been wearing a uniform without even realizing it. You might be new to New York, but I think you have the style down better. You want to consult on an interview outfit for me?"

Lucy's eyes lit with the same gleam Ellie had seen in them when the TV host of the reigning home decorating show had walked past them in the building lobby the previous week. "Yes. I'm telling you right now, no black." She leaned over their partition and lowered her voice. "What's your budget?"

"Nonexistent," Ellie admitted. Fledgling editors got paid squat, and chances were she'd be in between paychecks pretty soon. "I don't have a trust fund or a sugar daddy, so I've got about fifty dollars to donate to the cause."

Lucy's eyes widened and then narrowed as if she were studying Ellie's measurements. "Doesn't matter. I can make it work. When do you need it by?"

"My next interview is in three days. Is that too soon?"

"There is no such thing as too soon in doing something about your wardrobe. I'll get on it."

"Thanks, Lucy."

"Anything for you, peach."

Lucy popped back down, and Ellie turned her attention to her computer, hesitating before opening her current proofreading assignment. Amberly was making sure to pile on more busywork than any two people could do, but since Meredith hadn't officially taken her off of slush pile duty, Ellie wouldn't feel guilty about checking it. If Max Crowe had been shoved in there, who knew what else she might find?

The practical part of her that always bought black dresses resisted the idea of searching for a project she would never see published, but she ignored that voice for twenty minutes while she sifted through a half dozen cover letters from hopeful writers. Once again, they showed way more enthusiasm than skill. Giving up, she clicked to open her proofing work, but the appearance of the formulaic crime novel on her screen snuffed out her initiative faster than the nosy neighbor had killed the main character's husband. It depressed her that she'd guessed the murderer by page three. She scrolled to the end to check. Yeah, it was the neighbor.

She shut the document again. Blah.

The only thing she felt like doing was chatting with Max. The clock said it would be late evening in Afghanistan, but she'd caught Max at odd hours before. And it wouldn't be so late that he was asleep yet, probably. She'd come to rely on their evening chats to help her unwind after doing a few more hours' work at home. She eyed the clock again and pulled up his e-mail address.

To: Max Crowe
From: Eleanor H
Subject: I want it now!

So, no blog post this morning. You trying to torture your reading public or something? In some cultures, late blog posts are grounds for shunning. Like with the Amish. If you have a late blog post, that's it. You're shunned. Have anything to say for yourself?

She hit send and opened up the proof pages with a sigh. She wished for a half second that she was the kind of person who didn't care about doing a meticulous job. She could fly through the pages and send them pinging back to Amberly at warp speed, but she did care, especially about words and most especially about words she had any kind of responsibility over.

She was three pages into her work and already entertaining herself by guessing—correctly most of the time—what the characters would say next when a message alert showed up for her personal e-mail.

To: Eleanor H
From: Max Crowe
RE: I want it now!

I was not aware the Amish blogged. Or did anything with computers. Or electricity, actually. But you're the one who lives in Pennsylvania (right?), so I guess you know more about the Amish than I do. However, I feel the need to do some investigative reporting on the truth about the underground Amish blogging community.

That will have to wait though because . . .

A story I've been working on has suddenly found life when I was pretty sure it was dead, so I think I'm about to be pretty busy.

And I would tell you about it, but I don't want to jinx it.

Get back to work.

To: Max Crowe
From: Eleanor H
RE: I want it now!

How do you know I'm even at work?

To: Eleanor H
From: Max Crowe
RE: I want it now!

In every time zone in the country, you'd still have to be at work. If you have a desk job. Which you do, right?

To: Max Crowe
From: Eleanor H
RE: I want it now!

Fine, yes, you guessed it. I have a desk job. But what makes you think I'm in America right now? You think you're the only one who gets to take far-flung countries by storm? Maybe I'm in some exotic location too.

To: Eleanor H
From: Max Crowe
RE: I want it now!

Exotic. Too.

Wait a minute. Do you think I'm still in Afghanistan?

To: Max Crowe
From: Eleanor H
RE: I want it now!

I guess I don't now. Are you in . . . New York? Back at the paper?

Ellie sat back, her eyes glued to the screen. She scrolled through their conversations in her mind. Had Max ever said he was in Afghanistan? She'd assumed all along that he was there, but the more she thought about it, the more she realized he'd never said so.

To: Eleanor H
From: Max Crowe
RE: I want it now!

I've been back in New York for almost two months. I need to touch the soil of the motherland—or the Manhattan pavement—every now and then. My editor was worried I was getting burned out, so he pulled me home, and I've been blogging for the paper instead. Should be getting a new assignment soon, but this was the right break at the right time.

If Amberly and Paige had tied Ellie to her desk chair and spun her for five minutes straight, she couldn't have felt more dizzy.

He was here, at his home base.

Her home base. He might be mere blocks away from her in the *Metro News* offices at that very moment.

She gripped the edge of her desk and took a deep breath. It was stupid to let that unsettle her, but there'd been this small part of her imagination that had spun out dozens of scenarios where she and Max e-mailed for months, and then when he came back to the States, she would admit that she lived right there in the city too, and they would make plans to meet, maybe grab lunch one day . . .

Ha. That was the most boring of her daydreams. She had about fifty variations of the final scene in *You've Got Mail* in her head, one where she was standing in Central Park and he came and found her. Or there was the scene where she would wander past the coffee cart outside of the newspaper building and bump into him, and she would give him a shy smile and say, "Hi, Max." Confusion would ripple over his face but fascination too as he tried to understand the instant connection he felt to her, a stranger. Then, later that night, she would e-mail him and confess who had said hello to him, and he would beg to see her again.

She'd laughed at herself every time she'd caught herself in one of these daydreams. Max didn't have more than a handful of clues about who she was. He'd never asked her for a picture or hinted that he enjoyed her as more than one of his many e-mail friends. She breathed deeply again, drawing in the scent of copy paper and the burned-popcorn smell drifting from the break room. The situation was no different now than it had been five minutes ago when she'd thought he was safely across the world in Afghanistan. He hadn't been imagining them meeting on his end of their chats.

But . . . She frowned. She thought he'd spent so much time chatting with her at night because he needed the distraction while he was in Afghanistan. What reason did he have for talking to her every night when he had New York City at his feet and no trigger-happy insurgents keeping him shut up inside? Did he just like talking to her? Or was he some kind of hermit with social anxiety?

This was stupid. There couldn't be anything less helpful than asking herself questions only he knew the answers to. But it all still felt suddenly different, and she needed to think about why and if she wanted to change something about that. For once, she was glad she had a pile of proofing to do. Maybe her brain could work out what was bothering it while she focused on comma abuse.

Chapter 7

Ellie dropped her gym bag on the table and booted up her laptop. No new messages waited from Max. Fair enough. It was her turn, really. And after her evening workout, with an extra thirty minutes on the treadmill, she'd figured out why she was off balance. Maybe.

In Afghanistan, Max had been possible. She could make up whatever stories about him she wanted, invent as many ways for them to run into each other as she liked, play out the possibilities to infinity if she wanted to. Because *none* of it could be put to the test. Each scenario was as likely as any other scenario while he was that far away.

But Max being here? That meant the first hint of impossibility. Meeting him could be put to the test, and every daydream could evaporate. The punch to her gut his "I'm in New York" e-mail had delivered was nothing less than reality sinking in.

But she'd still found herself drifting into a couple more daydreams at the gym. Maybe she really would just bump into him somewhere, like that very gym, even. He looked like a guy who kept in shape. But when she'd caught herself checking out the cardio room to see if he was there, she'd realized it was time for her to make a decision. She could drive herself crazy looking for him everywhere she went, or she could own up and tell him that Big City, USA, was the same big city he occupied, and she could see what happened. She pulled up his last e-mail and stared at it for a full five minutes before she decided what to say.

To: Max Crowe
From: Eleanor H
RE: I want it now!

I didn't realize you were in New York. I just assumed you were still overseas. Now I've got a paradigm shift happening in my head. I live in Manhattan. Seems strange to think you're rattling around here too.

It only took about fifteen minutes before he IM'd her.

MC: You're kidding. You're right here in the city?
EH: Yeah.
MC: That's hilarious. I really thought you were in Boston or something. I guess I wasn't thinking Big City enough.
EH: :-)

She didn't know what to say. *Where do you live?* Yeah, right. He'd probably worry that she was going to knock on his door in twenty minutes flat. *I walk by the newspaper offices all the time.* Nope. That sounded like a hint that he should invite her to meet up. So a smiley face it was. She pictured a whole conversation on her side in emoticons because every word she thought about typing suddenly felt wrong.

MC: Now that you've confessed your true location, can you tell me your real job too?
EH: If you had all the facts, what would we talk about? Half our conversations are you guessing the details.
MC: What would we talk about? Books, art, movies, food. You know, the stuff we've been talking about for 99% of the time we talk that I'm NOT guessing your details.

Ellie didn't want to tell him her job. He'd immediately realize she was the one who'd rejected his book. Or maybe he'd suddenly want to spend all their conversations picking her brain about publishing, something that happened often when aspiring writers discovered what she did. They all wanted an in, and she'd already slammed Hutton's door shut on him. Even if he wasn't a little bit mad at her over that, publishing was her least favorite subject at the moment.

She changed the subject completely.

EH: Are you from here originally?

MC: Nope. Indiana. Went to Columbia and stayed because I loved it.

EH: Me too. I'm from Michigan, but I've been here six years now, and I can't imagine living anywhere different.

MC: Let's have a New York–off.

EH: A wha . . . ?

MC: I'm going to test you, see if you really love the city or if you're one of the pretenders she'll eventually spit out.

EH: Bring it.

MC: Best soul food?

EH: Sylvia's. Try harder.

MC: Best bookstore?

EH: The Strand. Seriously? This is supposed to be hard? My turn. Best museum?

MC: The MOMA.

EH: Correct. Also acceptable: the Guggenheim. The question of all questions: best pizza?

MC: Trick question. Every pizza shop on every corner in every neighborhood. The signs say so!

EH: Correct. I guess you've got your bona fides.

*MC: *Takes bow.* You too. We're going to have to call it a draw.*

Ellie leaned back and smiled at the screen, pressing her hands against her stomach to stop its fluttering. She was half hoping the next words to pop up would be him suggesting that they meet at one of the restaurants or museums they'd just dueled over. What would she say if he did?

She hadn't dated much, really. Every now and then she'd met a guy at a publishing event, soirees thrown to launch books or celebrate award nominations. She'd met a couple at the gym too. None of it amounted to much. She'd dated one guy for two months and another for three. The first one was more committed to his career than he was to another human being. The second told her she was too hard to get to open up.

She'd wanted to give him a big "Duh" over that. For her whole life, people had been leaving her. She'd learned the hard way not to attach.

She thought back to her earlier realization at the gym. She'd gotten it completely wrong. When she'd thought Max was in the wilds of Afghanistan, attachment was *im*possible. He was there and nothing could happen. And now he might suggest a face-to-face. And that meant *anything* could happen. Like attachment.

She wanted him to suggest grabbing coffee together so they could argue over the merits of their favorite cafés like she wanted the old version of her job back—with an ache that hurt like a side cramp after running too hard on the treadmill.

It was a scary feeling. And it made her very sure it was the last thing she wanted him to type after all.

Max is typing.

She eyed the warning with a dread she usually reserved for the sharp staccato sound of Amberly's heels clicking toward her desk.

MC: Do you work anywhere near Eighth and Fortieth?

That was the address of the *Metro* offices. He was going to suggest meeting up. A vague sense of carsickness washed over her, and her pulse picked up.

MC: Maybe we could grab lunch, and I can use my powers of journalistic observation to gather more clues about what you really do.

Her hands hovered over the keyboard to type a response. She frowned when she realized they had a tiny tremor.

Yes, do it.

She didn't know whose voice was in her head urging her to agree, but it definitely wasn't her common sense. It sounded like something Lucy would say.

Maybe Ellie *should* say yes. It would be so unlike her, but Ed had been pushing her toward greater risk taking, and Meredith was flinging her out of the nest with vicious force. Still, she hesitated. She'd rather be free and clear of Hutton first. She wanted it not to matter anymore. If she could say that she'd quit because Meredith had made her reject *Walking Home*, maybe he wouldn't hold it against her.

MC: You there?

EH: Sorry, yeah.

MC: Lunch?

EH: Sure. We can do that sometime. I should go now. I have more "things to fix" before I crash out for the night.

MC: Did . . . I cross some invisible boundary?

Yes.

EH: No. It's just getting late, that's all.

MC: Right. Okay.

* * *

Ellie pushed harder than ever the next day. She flew through the proofing Amberly sent her and skimmed two dozen entries in the slush pile. It didn't help keep her mind off the conversation with Max and the fact that she'd been a total weirdo about it.

She had to fix it. She couldn't say she'd rather not meet up with him, that their online chats were enough. That would underscore her rejection of him. She could say yes, they should meet up. And then it might be amazing and they'd be *You've Got Mail 2.0*. Or maybe have good chemistry as friends. But that felt like a consolation prize.

Worst of all, maybe he would find her odd and awkward. Because she was. Painfully so. It came from living in her head too much. Coworkers who got to know her loved her. But it took time—more than a lunch, anyway—to see past her shyness.

She'd worried her stomach into such a tight knot by dinnertime that she couldn't eat more than a yogurt with an iffy expiration date. She didn't change her chat status from "invisible." She was hiding. It was lame, but she still didn't change it.

She dragged herself into work Thursday morning. There was so much less to look forward to when she didn't have a talk with Max waiting at the end of the day. *How had that happened so fast?*

"You got my e-mail?" Lucy appeared over the cubicle wall and grinned at her.

Ellie blinked. What? E-mail? "Uh, yes?"

Lucy sighed. "So you didn't see my e-mail. I thought you read it and were impressed with how fast I pulled an outfit together for you. Allow me to summarize: I've got one, and you're going to look amazing in it."

"You just improved my morning 2,000 percent. Can I see?"

Lucy disappeared for a moment and bobbed back up to hand Ellie a shopping bag, proclaiming it was from the Love Me Twice consignment shop. "Open it," she urged her. "I think you're going to love it."

Ellie peeked inside, a whisper of excitement loosening her stomach knot as she caught a glimpse of sky. She pulled out a light-blue wrap dress with white piping around the neckline. "Whoa. This is really cute."

"There's more. Look in the bottom of the bag."

Ellie's eyes widened, but she did as directed. Out came a red bead necklace and red, sling-back, peep-toe heels. Her mouth dropped open, and she looked back and forth between the shoes and Lucy. She did it so many times Lucy giggled.

"There's no way you did this for fifty dollars," Ellie said. "And I kind of don't care. I love it."

"You're right. You owe me fifteen more dollars. That got the necklace and the dress. The shoes are mine. They're probably a half size too big, but they should work fine. Just don't scuff them."

"I won't. Oh my gosh, I owe you big time. Thank you so much."

"Don't get too excited. It might not look right. If the dress doesn't fit, just put the red accessories on with one of your black dresses, but do a vampy lip and something besides a low ponytail."

"It'll look good. Thank you. I already feel way more confident about tomorrow."

"If you really want to thank me, ace the interview and quit on Meredith without any notice."

Ellie grinned and promised, but Lucy's joke reminded her that she had to clear a longer lunch with Meredith in case tomorrow's interview ran late too.

She made the long walk to Meredith's office. Paige smiled at her from Ellie's old desk. Ellie imagined it was the kind of smile the winning actresses gave the losing actress when they bumped into each other at the after parties.

"What do you need, Ellie?" Paige asked. Even with her smile, it didn't sound polite.

"I need to clear a long lunch with Meredith tomorrow." She jerked her head in the direction of Meredith's office. Meredith looked up, and her eyes narrowed before she went back to the papers in front of her.

Ellie stifled a sigh. So now her boss wasn't even speaking to her?

"Again?" Paige picked up the phone and paged Meredith. "I'll ask, but she's really busy right now. Don't know if she has time to sign off on something like that."

Ellie fought an eye roll at Paige's posturing. It was a mean-girl tactic she'd seen since middle school. It was brazen and ridiculous for Paige to try to create the illusion of a scarcity of their boss's time when they could both see Meredith plainly through the glass wall ten feet away.

"Ellie wants to take a long lunch tomorrow," Paige said. Her tone suggested it was the stupidest request she'd ever had to run by Meredith.

Ellie watched Meredith's face tighten as she barked something into the receiver and plunked down the phone. Paige winced and hung up. "She said no, you can't have a long lunch tomorrow. Sorry." Her tone was completely unapologetic.

Ellie gave her a clipped nod and turned toward her desk, refusing to look Meredith's way as she did. Paige's phone rang behind her, and a second later, Paige called, "Stop."

Ellie turned around with her arms crossed. "What, Paige?"

"Meredith changed her mind. She said you can have an extra hour."

Ellie nodded and walked off again, too frustrated by their game-playing to offer a polite thank you. If she'd needed a last straw, that had been it. She'd rock her interview tomorrow.

Chapter 8

To: Eleanor H
From: Max Crowe
Subject: Do-over

Hi. You've been quiet the last two days. I feel like that's probably on me. Sorry about suggesting we meet up. I thought I'd better clarify that I'm not an Internet weirdo or anything. I think if you Google me, you won't find an arrest record. (Uh, if you do, let me know. Probably someone I forgot to pay off somewhere.) (Kidding. I swear.) Anyway, just wanted to make sure you understood the point of my invitation, which is this: I don't get a chance to meet many of my online pen pals, but every now and then I'm on assignment where they are, and I always try to meet and buy that friend coffee and pass a pleasant hour together. All my NYC friends are also in-real-life friends, so a New York pen pal is a new thing for me. Guess I didn't think about how my invitation might be perceived. Dumb on my part. So I hereby propose that we go back to our online anonymity, broken up only by periodic debates about our personal best-of-New-York votes. So don't stress, okay?

The message came in as Ellie reached to turn off her bedside lamp. Reading Max's words didn't make Ellie feel any better. There was nothing that would make her feel better until she made a decision about what she wanted. Anything Max said or failed to say would only bump up against her indecision and increase her paralysis. She loathed herself for it, but the only thing she could think to do was lock down a new job and make herself free to tell Max who she was and why she'd gone looking for him. Then they could sit down at a café somewhere and see if they could be friends. Or more . . .

Which was the part that terrified her—the wanting more and the ridiculous crush she should be too grown-up to have. It felt so ninth grade. She fell asleep imagining a walk with Max hand in hand through Central Park.

When her alarm woke her the next morning, she pulled the blue dress from her closet and smiled. She warmed up her curling iron for the first time in over a year and wrinkled her nose when she realized her eyeliner was still sharp from disuse.

An hour later, she had a hand on the doorknob when she paused and sat down in front of her laptop.

To: Max Crowe
From: Eleanor H
RE: Do-over

I'm not ignoring you. Remember how I said I fix things? That suddenly got complicated in the last two days. But I'll be back around soon to argue about the best of New York. We should probably start with cheesecake.

By the time she reached the Hutton building, she was a nervous but giddy wreck. She'd caught a lot of admiring glances on the subway. Maybe she was hyperalert because she felt so different without her black dress uniform, but it wasn't like her to invent that kind of attention for herself, which led her to believe she really was collecting approving smiles all the way to work.

She stepped off the elevator on her floor, and the Hutton receptionist glanced up with her practiced "good morning" smile. It stretched into a genuine smile when she saw Ellie. "Love the dress," she called as Ellie passed her with a wave.

Ellie collected a half dozen more compliments on the short walk to her desk. She sat down and dove right into the proofreading waiting for her. Five minutes later, Lucy's head poked into her cubicle, and she promptly squealed.

"Stand up! Let me see! You look amazing. I'm amazing! *I* didn't even know I was this good," she said, signaling for Ellie to twirl, which she did with a laugh.

"Yes, you're amazing. Maybe I should hire you as my personal stylist," Ellie said, glancing down at the red shoes. "Also, I'm probably stealing these."

"It's okay. I know where you work."

"For now," Ellie said, grinning.

"Feeling confident, hmm?" Lucy asked, smiling back. "You should. They'll be lucky to have you."

The irritating rhythm of Paige's high heels reached them, and Lucy's smile faded as she ducked around the cubicle to her side. Ellie turned back to her computer. The heels paused near her desk, but when Ellie didn't look up, the clicking continued down the hall. She had read not quite half a page when her phone rang on the internal line.

"This is Ellie," she said.

"Meredith needs you. Now." Paige hung up before Ellie could respond.

Ellie pushed back from her desk, stood up, smoothed her dress, and sat down again. She stood up and forced herself to walk back to Meredith's office.

"You wanted to see me?" Ellie said.

"Yes." Meredith smiled. Ellie blinked, unused to seeing the smile directed at her. "You're taking a long lunch today, correct?"

"Yes," Ellie answered, drawing the word out until it was almost a question.

"May I ask where you're going?"

Meredith's tone was so courteous it made Ellie blink again. How was she supposed to answer that? *A job interview so I can ditch you?* Not likely. "I have an appointment," she said, deciding on vagueness.

Meredith's smile suggested she'd been reading Ellie's calendar. "I'm guessing based on your appearance that it's either a date or a job interview. If it's the latter, I'm sorry to hear that you're thinking about leaving us, but I want you to know that you can expect a glowing reference from me."

Ellie took a step back and caught herself. This conversation couldn't be weirder if Meredith had suddenly suggested they take a girl day at the spa together. Ellie offered a weak "Thank you."

"So you'll be leaving around eleven thirty?"

"Yes, if that's still okay."

"Of course. Feel free to leave a little earlier if you need to." Meredith's smile had stretched so wide at this point that it was sliding from "encouraging" to "feral." She seemed to recognize the confusion in Ellie's face because she toned it down and nodded toward the door. "I don't want to keep you, but please don't have any concerns about using my name as a reference."

Ellie mumbled another thank you and beat a retreat to her desk, collecting another crop of compliments on her outfit as she went. She sat back down to her proofreading assignment, but she stared at it without seeing anything. She'd expected Meredith to be glad she was quitting, but she hadn't expected her to be nice about it. So weird.

She tried to push it out of her head. By the time the clock edged past eleven, her stomach had pretzled so hard she couldn't focus on proofreading. She needed to calm down if she didn't want to walk into *Tasteful Travel* wound tighter than a playground swing. She ate a piece of chocolate from her emergency stash. It wasn't enough.

Forget relaxation. That wouldn't happen. She needed to focus, to remind herself of why she was going to the interview in the first place. She pulled up Max's column on the *Metro News* site. Her pulse steadied when she saw that a new post had gone up today, and she soon fell inside his article on how the same hopes that drove the merchants in the crowded Kabul bazaar drove the owners of every Manhattan bodega. She was so deep into the story, in fact, that she missed the warning click of heels and jumped at the sound of Paige clearing her throat.

"What are you doing?"

Heat crept into Ellie's cheeks, and she slid her glance to Max's post on her monitor. "I was just doing some research."

Paige waved away Ellie's half-truth. "No, I mean, aren't you supposed to be somewhere else? That isn't here?"

Ellie checked the time. It was almost eleven thirty. "Uh, I have a few minutes still." The magazine offices weren't far.

"No, you should probably go. Really. You don't want to be late for your thing. Meredith is fine with you leaving right now."

"Okay," Ellie said slowly, a tickle in her chest telling her something wasn't right. "Thanks. I'll head out."

"Great," Paige said. She waved and headed back down the hall.

What in the world? If Meredith was in a hurry to rush Ellie out, Ellie would make a point of hanging around as long as possible. She moved at half speed to double-check her satchel. *Copy of résumé? Check. Emergency tissue? Check. Lip gloss? Check.* She pulled the tube out and applied some. Slowly. Then she decided she didn't like the coverage and wiped it off and did it again.

She'd run out of ways to delay when Amberly hustled past her desk, shooting a panicked look in Ellie's direction as she headed up to reception. Nothing short of building security could remove Ellie from her cubicle now. Not two minutes later, she heard Amberly again. She was walking back even faster than normal, two guys in her wake.

The guys drew closer. They were both youngish. One was dark-haired in his early thirties. He smiled politely as he listened to Amberly. But the other guy, the one with golden hair, captured every bit of her attention and all of her breath.

Max Crowe.

She'd stared at his profile photo often enough to be sure. She glanced at her monitor, but there was no doubt that the face smiling next to his column was the same face about to pass her desk. She stood and gripped the top of her cubicle wall. She wanted to collapse into her chair and step out to meet him at the same time, but the impulses canceled each other out, and she froze instead.

Panic flickered through her. Had he figured out her identity and tracked her down? His expression didn't suggest that he was looking for anyone as much as he was cataloging everything he saw and absorbing the details. His head turned toward her, and her calves tensed as if they were going to propel the rest of her to a dive for safety no matter what her brain said. Max's eyes met hers, and he smiled, although it bore the tinge of a question as he noted her expression. A gleam of curiosity lit his eyes, but Amberly placed her hand on his arm and drew him past quickly, chattering to both Max and the other man about the proud history of Hutton.

Ellie watched them until they got to the far end of the hall and turned into Meredith's office. When Paige shut the door behind them, it snapped the invisible thread tying Ellie's gaze to Max Crowe, and she sat down on her office chair. Hard.

Why was Max here? If Amberly was talking up Hutton, it could only mean they were trying to sell him on the idea of publishing here. Authors came in often—after they had books under contract. But they only came in before a contract was signed when one of the editors was trying hard to woo them away from someone else . . .

Ellie clicked through her contact list at warp speed, finding the number she needed in seconds. She stabbed it out on the phone, her finger throbbing seven digits later. *Please, please, please be there.*

"This is Andrew."

Ellie's grip on the phone tightened. *Thank goodness.* "Hi, Andrew. It's Ellie Hanover at Hutton."

"Ellie! Great to hear from you. How are you?"

"Great. Sorry to bug you, but I'm checking in to see if you read that manuscript I sent over to you."

"I did. And it was so excellent. But next time, could you give me a week or two to have it exclusively before you tell anyone else about it? I'll give you my firstborn. Wait, no, he cries a lot. If the second one is quieter, you can have that one instead."

"You can keep your kids, Andrew. I *did* give you an exclusive." Her pulse kicked into overdrive. Her hunch was right.

"Oh." Andrew seemed to consider that for a moment. "I guess it's my bad luck that someone else pulled it out of the slush pile at the same time I was looking at it."

"What do you mean?" Ellie asked, trying to keep her curiosity sounding within normal bounds.

"I e-mailed the agent a few days ago to let him know we were interested, but he said they already had an offer. So now I think we're on the verge of a bidding war. You really don't know who the other bidder is?"

She did now. "This is the first I've heard of a bidding war," she said. "Good luck. I have a feeling things will go your way."

She was about to make sure of it.

Chapter 9

"WHERE ARE YOU GOING?" AMBERLY asked as Ellie passed her.

Ellie didn't answer.

"You can't go in there," Paige called as Ellie passed her.

Ellie didn't answer. She could see the back of Max's head through Meredith's window, and Meredith herself sat smiling with the charm she deployed when she wanted something.

Ellie rapped twice on the door and pushed it open over Paige's protests. Meredith's smile stiffened when she saw Ellie in the doorway. "Can I help you?"

"Sorry I'm late," Ellie said, her own smile in place. "Got caught in some work."

"Don't you have somewhere else to be?"

"No. I changed my plans when I realized you'd forgotten to include me in the meeting. Don't worry. My schedule is clear now."

Max's and his agent's heads had turned as soon as she'd walked in, but now Darren's mouth hung slightly open, and that curious gleam had reappeared in Max's eyes.

Meredith cleared her throat. "It's better if you leave. Your poor judgment has caused Mr. Crowe some unnecessary frustration, and I'm doing my best to show him that not everyone at Hutton shares your editorial views."

Ellie didn't even blink. She'd expected Meredith to say something exactly like that. "It's true we don't share the same editorial views." She looked Max in the eye. "I loved your book, Mr. Crowe. I'm the one who wanted to pitch it to the board."

Darren's expression was that of a man who had just listened to an entire conversation in Swahili. He turned to Meredith. "I'm sorry. Who is this?"

"I'm Ellie Hanover," she said, stepping forward and offering her hand for a shake. Darren accepted it, and she offered it to Max next. His hand closed over hers, warm and strong, his palm slightly rough. It felt like a hand that did things besides type at a keyboard all day. She wanted to hold on to it, memorize the feel of it, but his eyes had widened the tiniest bit, and she let go and stepped back so fast she almost yanked her hand away.

Darren seemed to be finding his footing. "Ellie Hanover? You're the one who sent me the original rejection."

Meredith cleared her throat. "That was a huge mistake on her part, and she's been handled accordingly. Go back to your desk, Ellie. We'll talk about this later."

"I want to talk about it now," Ellie said, moving to the side of the desk so no one had to twist to look at her. She almost regretted it when she could feel Max's steady gaze. It pressed all over her skin, making it harder for her to breathe. "I brought your book to Meredith, and she didn't want to discuss it. But I thought it was genius. Honestly. And it killed me to have to send that rejection."

Darren smiled. "It was the nicest rejection that came in."

Ellie inhaled, trying to loosen the tightness in her chest, and pushed her next words out on a wish that Max would hear what she was really saying. "The thing is, I fix things. And nothing could be more broken than that book not seeing the light of day. So I sent an e-mail to an acquaintance at Beacher."

Darren's eyes widened, but Max's narrowed so far she could barely see the glint of their blue.

"Don't sign here," she said. "You won't get the editor who loves what you do. You'll get Meredith, who doesn't get you."

A flood of red swept over Meredith's face. "How dare you—"

"Don't worry, I quit, so you can't fire me," Ellie said, too angry to be scared of the gathering storm in her boss's—ex-boss's—face. She met Max's shocked eyes. "You guys should call Andrew Bale. I'm not sure it's possible for him to love *Walking Home* as much as I do, but I think it'll be pretty close."

She turned to leave, feeling like someone had forgotten to give her a parting line in the weird scene that had just played out. She stopped at the door and smiled at Max. "You write otherness like no one I've ever read."

She closed the door behind her, barely registering Paige's stunned expression, and hurried back to her desk to grab her purse. If she hustled, she could still make it to her interview ten minutes late, and suddenly that interview had become a necessity. If Meredith had security keep her out when she got back, maybe Lucy would be willing to pack up her desk and drop the boxes by her house after work.

She snatched up her purse and almost ran to the elevator when a voice behind her stopped her.

"Eleanor?"

She turned. Max stood there, a half smile on his face. She gripped her purse strap so hard her knuckles whitened.

"It's you, isn't it? Eleanor H? Ellie Hanover?" His smile stretched wider when she didn't deny it. "I warned you; I'm an amazing investigative journalist."

She couldn't help but laugh. "I gave you some giant clues."

"Thank you for that, by the way. I've spent the last two days thinking of all the questions I could ask you to convince you to open up a little more, but I felt less like a reporter and more like a . . ."

"Like a what?"

"Um. No need to bring the world *stalker* into this conversation."

"You just did."

He smiled. "Let's pretend I didn't. And then change the subject."

"To what? The weather?" she asked, an answering smile creeping up on her despite the clock ticking past any chance she had of salvaging her interview and despite the fact that she had just become unemployed a minute before.

"No, to bombs."

That stopped her short. "Bombs?"

He nodded and stepped closer to her, glancing around the reception area. She followed his gaze and realized they'd attracted an audience. Her cheeks heated.

"Bombs," he repeated in a lowered voice. "I've had some experience with them. Once, a friend I'd known for two weeks threw himself on top of a guy who was trying to detonate an IED to blow up the truck I was riding in. The friend was an interpreter, and he jumped off the truck and tackled the bomber before he could set it off with the phone he'd rigged."

"Wow," Ellie said, because she had no idea what kind of reaction was warranted.

"Yeah. Wow. But that guy had backup. A bunch of soldiers swarmed down after him and subdued the bomber. You, on the other hand, didn't throw yourself on the bomber; you threw yourself on the bomb." His smiled faded, and his voice grew quiet, flickers of guilt wavering in his irises. "No one's ever done something like that for me before. Thank you."

The heat in her cheeks intensified. "You're welcome," she said, shifting on her feet before forcing herself to be still.

"It's the strangest thing," he said slowly. "I've never met you, and yet I feel like I know you so well that—"

He broke off and glanced around the reception area again.

"That . . . what?" she prompted him again, needing to know with the same urgency that she needed air how he would finish that sentence.

He touched her elbow so lightly she shouldn't have felt it, yet heat shot all the way down her arm to her palm, and it tingled. "Would you like to get coffee, maybe? Like right now?"

"What about . . . ?" She waved her hand in Meredith's direction.

"That's not going to happen."

"Then yes to coffee." She suddenly couldn't care less about her job interview. Coffee with Max took no convincing at all.

"You pick; I'll pay, seeing as you don't have a job anymore." The guilt was thick in his voice again.

They stepped into the elevator, and when the doors closed, she turned to face him. "I should tell you something."

"You really do repair small electronics, and this was your side job?"

"No." She smiled because it felt good to speak the truth out loud. "I started hating my job about a month ago. So much. I don't even have words for how much. So I appreciate your gratitude, but I feel better than I have in weeks."

Relief crossed his face, but before he could speak, the elevator stopped and let new passengers on, so they rode to the lobby in silence. Three times she snuck a glance at Max, and each time she caught him doing the same thing. The fourth time it happened, she couldn't fight the laugh that bubbled up. She snuck one more glance and found him grinning.

In the lobby, he turned to her with a questioning look. She pointed to the cart outside. "The joe is okay, but then you drink it on a bench in the park, and suddenly it's excellent."

"Can't think of a better way to spend lunch."

"Meredith was probably going to take you guys out to somewhere five star on Hutton's dime, wasn't she?"

He shrugged. "I'm already having a better lunch."

They ordered their drinks, and she led him to her favorite bench. She traced the rim of her cup, too nervous to drink it. "You said you know me so well that . . . what? You didn't finish in there."

"That I knew exactly how you would react." He rested his elbows on his knees and rolled his cup back and forth between his palms. "I told you I've made friends all over the world because of my reporting." He shrugged. "Enemies too. I wasn't kidding about keeping up with a lot of them through regular e-mails and chats. It helped pass the time when I was out in the field, definitely. I go back and forth with people who could fill a bookshelf with stories about their misadventures, people who could order deaths with a phone call, and people who could buy and sell that building with their petty cash," he said, nodding at the Hutton offices. "Not one of them has ever made me want to haunt my computer while I waited for e-mails to come in. But you did."

He held her gaze, studying her with a tiny smile playing at one side of his mouth. "Is that just me?"

She shook her head, her heart pounding so hard she was sure he could hear the answer it was giving him from inside her chest. "It's not just you."

He nodded and drank from his cup, his expression thoughtful. "This is okay," he said finally. "But I know where to get an even better cup about a block up. We should try it sometime."

A smile untouched by nerves spread across her face. "Yes, we should."

He nudged her knee with his. "Like tomorrow."

She nodded. "Tomorrow."

"Good."

They both sipped their drinks and watched the taxis surge forward on the street in front of them until the light changed and brought them to a halt again. Silence had fallen between them, but it was the kind of silence that hummed with unspoken good things.

When the light turned green, Max cleared his throat. "You know that the day after tomorrow I'm going to invent another place we have to try. Just to be honest with you, I'm going to invent places to check out every day until you tell me no."

Warmth unfolded in her midsection and drifted all the way up to her cheeks. She smiled and nudged his knee with hers. "You're going to need a long list."

Chapter 10

Ellie lifted the top book from the box of advance copies and ran her finger over the raised letters of the title. *Walking Home.* She'd read the book more times than she could count now, but seeing it in hardback glory raised goose bumps on her arm. She flipped to the very back to the one page Max hadn't let her see before it had gone to press.

Acknowledgments

This book wouldn't have happened without the incredible people of Afghanistan. I witnessed their resiliency and spirit daily for two years. It was a privilege.

My agent, Darren Lansing, and I took a professional chance on each other when it didn't make sense for either of us, but working off of gut instinct has always served me well. It paid off in spades here. Thanks for championing my book.

And this book wouldn't be what it is if it hadn't been for my editor at Beacher Publishing, who also happens to be the love of my life, the incomparable Ellie Hanover. You are magic.

OTHER BOOKS AND AUDIO BOOKS
BY MELANIE JACOBSON

The List

Not My Type

Twitterpated

Smart Move

Second Chances

Painting Kisses

He Loves Me Not

by

JENNIFER K. CLARK

To all the river guides who share their adventures with us

Chapter 1

Kenedee stepped outside the small tin office building and shielded her eyes against the sweltering sun as she looked at the rocky cliffs surrounding Moab, Utah. They were a dark red—almost purple—as if they had a severe case of sunburn, which didn't seem all that unlikely this morning. It was just past eleven, and the temperature was already elbowing its way into the nineties. She let the heat soak into her long, brown hair. She didn't mind the scorching weather. The hotter it was, the more tourists seemed to find their way into the parking lot, and that was exactly what River Quest needed.

"Emma!" Kenedee yelled toward the storage shed, where a large flatbed trailer already held two rafts. "Your afternoon group canceled." Emma poked her head out from behind the trailer and stared at her in disbelief. "Someone in their group wrecked their mountain bike on one of the slick rock trails, and they aren't up for any more adventures."

"Are you kidding me?" Emma threw an oar on the back of the trailer. "That makes two days in a row! I really wanted to ride the river today."

Gravel crunched behind Kenedee, and she turned and watched Andrew and Dravin approach. Her eyes slid across Andrew and settled on Dravin. Despite his drawstring shorts and faded T-shirt, he somehow managed to look as though he'd just come from a photo shoot. She couldn't help but smile, but, ugh, she didn't look forward to telling him the news.

The brothers stopped in front of her. Dravin stuffed his hands in his pockets, and his lips pulled into a tight line. "Did I just hear our afternoon group canceled?"

"Unfortunately, yes." Kenedee hated to disappoint him, and it wasn't just because he was her boss. She couldn't deny that she was starting to fall for him. Maybe she should try to curb her feelings; after all, he didn't seem quite ready to start a relationship with her, though his secret deliveries of flowers said otherwise. She kicked her toe in the dusty gravel. Hopefully it wouldn't be too long before he admitted to giving them to her. A new bouquet mysteriously appeared on her desk almost every week. One had come with a plastic heart stuck in it, but there was never a note. She didn't need one. She had arrived early to work one day and had seen Dravin through the window as he'd placed the flowers on her desk. He was the last person she had suspected, but it was a pleasant surprise, nonetheless. And she completely understood why he needed to keep it a secret—at least for now.

She put her hand on his arm and tried to make the gesture one of comfort. "Don't worry about the cancelation. It's a hot day, and I'm sure we'll get a walk-in." It was the best she could do, but Dravin still frowned.

Andrew nudged himself between them. "If there's a walk-in, I get them." Like the average river guide, Andrew was kind of rough, passably handsome, and always joking around.

"No way!" Emma stepped forward, her face turning red, but she stopped when she saw the smirk on Andrew's face. He loved being on the river and always took the walk-ins, but he wouldn't take one from Emma—not after her regular daily had canceled.

"The new brochures came in," Kenedee said. "I'll have one of the warehouse boys run them around town. And I'll put a 10-percent-discount coupon on Facebook. That ought to bring in some business."

"See." Andrew clapped Dravin on the shoulder. "Kenedee always has things under control." His mouth turned up in a wide grin. That was the one thing Andrew had over Dravin—he was quick to smile, always looking on the bright side of things. But Kenedee had hoped to elicit that reaction from Dravin. Unfortunately, he only nodded and walked back to the office.

When they were alone, Emma nudged Kenedee. "Brochures and coupons—you're awesome. Hiring you was the best thing Dravin ever did for this business."

"That's because he wanted a secretary to book their expeditions and got a built-in accountant, janitor, head of marketing, and general manager too. I'm superwoman"—Kenedee looked down at her petite five-foot frame—"concentrated in a small package."

Emma chuckled. "And humility is your best quality." She nodded her head toward the office. "Come on; let's go inside. If I stay out here any longer, I'm going to melt."

The bell over the door rang as they walked into the air-conditioned room. Kenedee sat down at her desk behind the reception counter. She hadn't meant to brag. She just hoped Dravin saw her value. She glanced at the flowers on her desk. They had appeared that morning. Daisies—her favorite. Perhaps he did appreciate her. He just wasn't vocal about it.

Emma leaned on the reception counter and rolled her eyes at the flowers but didn't say anything. Instead, she pulled a Snickers out of her pocket and unwrapped it—her second one for the day. Somehow her body turned each piece of chocolate into sheer energy and muscle. As far as river guides went, Emma was as tough as any of the men. "We should ditch and go take a run ourselves," she said between bites.

"That'd be nice, but I can't. I'm putting the discount coupon on the web. Besides, there are benefits to hanging around here." Kenedee nodded toward the back office. "And he's sitting on the other side of that door."

Emma took another bite of her Snickers and stared lazily at the door. "Not Dravin again. Aren't you forgetting something?"

"Like what? He's hot. I'm single. He makes messes. I organize them. He sends me flowers, and I pretend I don't know where they come from. We're perfect for each other."

"Right. Go back to the 'I'm single' part. It's nice that you aren't tied down, but aren't you forgetting the tiny detail that Dravin is?"

"What? You mean Charlotte? Okay, he has a girlfriend, but that's a minor speed bump." Kenedee absentmindedly put her hand on the vase of flowers and turned it slightly.

"The daisies might not mean what you think." Emma took another bite and continued. "Maybe he's just trying to be a good boss. Or maybe he wants to brighten up the office." The door to the back room opened, and Emma clamped her mouth shut as Dravin walked out.

Kenedee smiled up at him. "I'm putting the coupon on Facebook right now."

He didn't react. Then she saw the cell phone at his ear. "All right," he said into it. "I'm coming out right now. See you in a second." He ended the call and walked outside without even glancing in Kenedee's direction. She pretended it didn't hurt.

Emma gave Kenedee a pointed look. "I bet you a candy bar she's outside waiting for him."

Kenedee didn't reply, but she walked over to the window and looked out.

"I was right, wasn't I?" Emma didn't move from the counter. "What's she wearing today?"

Charlotte's Hollywood-style fashions were always a topic of conversation. "A hot-pink strapless tank and a short ruffled skirt." Kenedee didn't mention that the outfit was fit for Rodeo Drive or that Charlotte's long, blonde hair and flawless smile complemented the pink ensemble perfectly. She turned away from the window. "I hate pink."

Emma wadded her candy wrapper into a tight ball and lobbed it across the room to the garbage can. Of course it hit its mark without even nicking the rim. "And if Dravin dated someone who wore purple, you would hate purple. Call me the bearer of bad news, but you've got to get over him." Kenedee ignored her, so Emma continued. "At least be realistic and pine after someone who isn't taken. How about one of the new river guides—Jackson or Luke? They're single, and you couldn't get closer to a Greek god in the flesh than Jackson."

"Yeah, and he flirts with every Barbie doll over the age of sixteen who steps foot in his raft. I think I need someone with a little more substance."

The bell over the door rang, and Kenedee looked up, hoping she would finally catch Dravin's smile, but it wasn't Dravin. It was Andrew. He reached into a side pocket on his cargo shorts, pulled out a mini Hershey's bar, and tossed it to Emma. "I just ran to the bank and thought of you when I saw their candy bowl."

"Thanks." Emma eyed the chocolate with appreciation.

"I grabbed one for you too." He handed a small Butterfinger to Kenedee. "You always have those peanut butter and banana sandwiches, so I thought you'd like this."

Kenedee usually didn't eat junk food, but Dravin had ignored her. She needed some chocolate consolation.

"There you go." Emma winked at her and gave a discreet nod in Andrew's direction. "A guy who goes to the bank and comes back with candy bars—I'd say that qualifies as someone with substance."

Kenedee gave her friend a warning look. It wasn't that she didn't like Andrew. He was funny and nice, and she enjoyed being around him, but there was something about Dravin's subtle flirting and secret deliveries that put him on a different plane from Andrew.

Andrew turned back to Kenedee with a shrug. "UPS just delivered our new life vests. If you have a minute, maybe you could help me label them."

Kenedee opened her mouth to answer, but Emma distracted her by grabbing a black marker from the overstuffed desk organizer and scribbling something on a piece of paper. Kenedee looked back at Andrew just as Emma stepped behind him and held up the paper. The words, *Bonus . . . He's single* were written in bold black letters with an arrow drawn underneath. The arrow was meant to point at Andrew, but it was clearly pointing at the water cooler. Andrew spun around, but Emma had already hidden the paper behind her back.

"Am I missing something here?" He looked back and forth between the girls.

Kenedee grabbed two more markers from her organizer and handed one to Andrew. "No. Emma is clearly out of her mind. Let's go label those vests."

Dravin and Charlotte still stood in the parking lot, and Charlotte had one hand wrapped around Dravin's back and the other intertwined in his dark hair. The image burned itself into Kenedee's mind. It should have confirmed that Dravin was off-limits, but it only made her more determined. Or maybe just irritated.

"Come on; it'll be fun," Charlotte said.

Dravin pulled Charlotte's hands off of him. "I can't leave work every time you want me to. Besides, I have a meeting with someone from Canyon Cliff Adventures."

Charlotte puffed out her bottom lip in a pout, then leaned forward and started kissing him.

Kenedee wasn't following Andrew anymore. She stood staring at Dravin, unable to make her feet move.

"Doesn't this change your mind?" Charolette said between kisses. She pulled his head down and trailed more kisses all the way from his ear down to his lips.

Dravin put his hands on her shoulders and pushed her back. "No." His voice was firm with an edge of irritation.

Charlotte's lip pouted out again. "Last chance. Andrew can take the meeting for you—"

"No, I can't," Andrew called over his shoulder. "I'm taking the shuttle up to the take-out to pick up Luke's group."

Kenedee smiled. Luke's group wasn't scheduled to come off the river for another three hours, but she admired Andrew for not caving in to Charlotte.

Dravin whispered something to Charlotte, then gently helped her into her car. A moment later, she revved the engine and peeled out of the parking lot.

Dravin turned to Kenedee. "Never fall in love while you're trying to start a business."

Kenedee wrinkled her brow. She didn't know what to think. He'd just given her flowers, then turned around and kissed Charlotte. Well, it was actually all Charlotte. Dravin *had* tried to push her away. But still. And was he hinting that he couldn't move forward, that the secret flower deliveries were going to continue indefinitely because he needed to put all of his focus on River Quest? Kenedee leveled her eyes on him. "I can see how that wouldn't work . . . unless you were to fall in love with someone in the business." She paused, then dropped her gaze to the ground, hoping to hide the heat creeping into her cheeks. "At least that way you could work together."

Dravin dipped his chin toward her. "That might not be a bad idea."

Kenedee felt her face flush even more.

"Did you post the discount coupon on the website?"

"Yes."

Dravin clapped a hand on her shoulder. "You're always on top of things around here. I don't know what I'd do without you."

She looked up and searched his brown eyes. For a moment, she hoped he would admit to giving her the flowers. Surely his gaze washing over her meant it wouldn't be too long. She craved it but cowered from it at the same time. It might be only a few weeks before she would be the one pressing kisses to his lips. At least she wouldn't be obnoxious about it. She wouldn't use those tender moments to get her way like Charlotte did. Each of her kisses would signify her commitment to him.

"I couldn't run this business without you," Dravin said. He patted her shoulder again and walked toward the office.

Kenedee frowned. "He patted me like a dog."

When Kenedee stepped into the large tin building used to house the rafting equipment, Andrew was already at work. He was sitting on the floor, marker in hand, carefully writing the words *River Quest* on the back of one of the life vests. When he was done, he set it aside and looked up at her. "Are you all right?"

Kenedee cleared her throat, trying to shrug off her emotions. "Yeah. Why do you ask?"

"Your face is red. You're not getting sunstroke, are you? Want me to grab you a cup of water?"

"No, I'm fine." She picked up a vest and began to label it.

"You don't need to do that." He reached over and put his hand on top of hers, stopping her writing. "You really don't have to help."

"But you asked me to."

He pulled the marker out of her hand and capped it. "I wanted to talk to you . . . privately."

"What about?" Kenedee's posture relaxed as she anticipated their usual topics of conversation. The condition of the river or the new brochure design—actually, anything would be a welcome relief as long as it cleared her thoughts of Dravin.

"Well . . ." Andrew paused and gave a quick, nervous glance around the building. "I wanted to talk to you about Dravin."

The air went out of Kenedee's lungs. "What about Dravin?"

He glanced around the room again. "I'm not asking you to do anything illegal—"

"Hasn't anyone warned you to never start a sentence that way?" Kenedee gave him a sidelong glance with her best I-hope-you're-kidding expression. Andrew didn't even crack a smile, and that worried her. He wasn't really contemplating something illegal, was he? "Andrew, what are you getting at?"

"Like I said, I'm not asking you to do anything wrong . . . well, according to the law . . . I just want to do something for Dravin today—for his own good. I want to run a little scam on him, and I need you to pull it off."

Chapter 2

"You told him no, right?" Emma stood next to the counter, drilling her eyes into Kenedee. "You know this is asking for trouble. Just tell me you didn't agree to scam Dravin."

"All right, I didn't agree to it." Kenedee tried to keep her gaze steady, but she couldn't.

Emma threw her hands in the air. "You're lying."

"Not completely. I didn't agree to it—at first." Kenedee glanced away. "It's not like we're doing anything illegal, and it really is for the best. Do you want to end up working for Canyon Cliff Adventures?"

"Of course not. I'm not the all-inclusive, jack-of-all-trades type of guide. I mean, they already offer jeep tours, horseback riding, and ATV and bike rentals. And now they want to offer river-rafting excursions? In the end, they'll offer everything but specialize in nothing. They're the Walmart of outdoor adventures."

"I don't want to work for them either," Kenedee said. "But that's what's going to happen unless we convince Dravin not to sell out to them."

Emma let out a sigh. "I never suspected River Quest was this bad off."

"We just had a slow start because we weren't open at the start of the season, and Dravin has a balloon payment coming due on his loan. And I'm talking like $26,000." Kenedee paused and wrinkled her nose in frustration. "Sadly, Canyon Cliff Adventures made an offer that will more than take care of it."

"Okay, I understand the predicament, especially when we get cancellations like we did today, but do you really think a scam is the best way to convince Dravin not to sell? Remember how Andrew's last hoax turned out."

Kenedee tried not to laugh. "You mean when he put on a ski mask and tried to scare Dravin? That was funny."

"Yeah, except for the part where Dravin called 911. Four squad cars showed up."

"It was still funny. And don't worry; nothing like that will happen this time. It'll work; you'll see."

The look in Emma's eyes said she wasn't convinced. "Any sane person would just sit down and have a reasonable conversation with Dravin. You know, use a little persuasion and twist his arm."

Kenedee wrapped a rubber band around a batch of brochures and tossed them on her desk. "Andrew tried that already. Apparently Dravin thinks selling is the only sure fix because he only has a couple of weeks to come up with the money."

"And this scam isn't going to solve the problem."

"Dangling the deal worth nine grand in front of him is only the ploy to get him to postpone the sale. In the meantime, Andrew will come up with the real cash. Dravin will still have to liquidate some assets to come up with the rest of the money, but as long as he doesn't sell out—"

"This is going to be more complicated than you think."

Kenedee waved her hand, batting away Emma's words like she was shooing a fly. "It's just a phone call and a little playacting. I'm a CEO of some company, and I'm arranging to send my two hundred employees on a rafting trip for some team-building experience. It's completely believable. I can even work in a Southern accent."

"And what if Andrew doesn't come through with his part? Dravin will default on the loan."

"Andrew's been working with multilevel marketing companies for weeks. And if even half of them agree to reward their top salesmen with a river trip—we'll still book over two hundred. He just needs a couple of weeks to clinch the deal."

Emma clucked her tongue. "Somehow, I don't think it will be that easy. Are you sure you aren't doing this just because it's Dravin—like this is some psycho way of getting more involved with him?"

Kenedee shifted in her seat. She didn't want to see River Quest go under, but ultimately, she had agreed to do it because of Dravin.

Typically, she would never put herself out like that, especially if it meant fooling someone, but it would help Dravin. This business was his life dream. He had worked hard to get it going, and she didn't want to see him lose it. "Kind of," Kenedee admitted.

"Kind of what?"

"I'm kind of doing this because of Dravin." She leaned forward and thumped her head against her desk a few times. "Does that make me bad?"

Emma shrugged. "Not bad. Pathetic comes to mind but not bad."

Kenedee went back to thumping her head again. It was pathetic. She hoped after they'd saved River Quest and Dravin knew the truth, he would look at her differently, admire her or something. It was dumb. He was just as likely to end up hating her. Or maybe he'd fire her for trying to con him.

Kenedee looked at Emma. "I need help, don't I?"

"That's what I'm here for. Friends are like a life vest. They keep you afloat when you get in deep water." A grin flashed across Emma's face, one that said she thought she was awesome for coming up with that analogy.

Kenedee threw a pen at her, but Emma ducked. "Okay, Life Vest, what do you suggest I do?"

"Don't go with this crazy idea. Just talk to Dravin. He'll probably admire you for being straightforward and voicing your concerns."

The phone rang, and both lines lit up. "Look at that," Kenedee said. "Two calls. Maybe my website coupon is working." She picked up the phone and hit line one. "River Quest. Will you please hold?"

Charlotte's sticky-sweet voice sounded from the other end. "No, I will not hold. Just put me through to Dravin. He's not answering his cell."

Kenedee held the phone away from her ear as if the voice on the other end was poison. "Maybe he's screening his calls. It's nothing personal. I'm sure he's just busy."

"Whatever. Just tell him I'm on the phone."

"Of course, just a moment." Kenedee purposefully pressed the hold button. "She can wait. It will be good for her."

"Is that Charlotte?"

Kenedee nodded and then answered line two. "River Quest. Can I help you?"

"This is John with Canyon Cliff Adventures. The person who can help me is Dravin Grant. Is he there?"

Kenedee looked at Emma and mouthed the words, "It's John from Walmart Adventures." She didn't know which of the two evils on the phone was worse, but she went ahead and transferred Charlotte's call to Dravin's office, then went back to John. "He is, but he's on the other line right now. Can I take a message?"

The man grunted in disappointment. "Tell him I can't make the meeting this afternoon. I don't know what his holdup is anyway. It's not like we aren't doing River Quest a favor." Obviously that part wasn't intended to be a part of the message.

Kenedee tightened her hand around the phone. "Would you like to reschedule the meeting, sir?"

"Yeah . . ." The man's voice became muffled as if he had covered the receiver with his hand. He began talking to someone else in the background. The words were faint and muted, but Kenedee could still make them out.

"Can you have the paperwork done by Friday? . . . Yes, up the offer five grand . . ." There was a rustling sound, and then the man was back. "My schedule is open Friday. Tell Dravin to give me a call, and we'll reschedule for then." There was a pause. "Did you get that?"

"Yes, sir."

The man hung up without another word.

Kenedee walked around the reception counter and handed the phone to Emma. "Will you stay in here and answer any calls?"

"Sure. Where are you going?"

The bell tinkled as she opened the door, and a blast of hot air hit her. She paused.

Emma took a step toward her. "Oh, no you don't!"

"I'm going to do it, Emma, so don't try to stop me. I can't just leave Dravin to the wolves—either one of them. I've got to do something."

Kenedee walked out, but not before she saw Emma's expression. It was a look that said, "I'll clear my schedule next week to help you look for a new job."

Chapter 3

THE SHUTTLE VAN WAS IN the parking lot when Kenedee stepped outside, which meant the scheme would have to wait. She needed to talk to Andrew first, but he would be busy now. The half-day morning group was chattering excitedly next to the River Quest van. Two tourists from France and a family from Kansas. They had only known each other for half a day, but they acted like old friends. The river did that; it had a way of bringing people together. It was one of the things she loved about it. She took a moment to visit with the group, then headed toward the warehouse.

The guys were already washing down the gear. Jackson was spraying off the life vests and hanging them on a long rope that stretched across one side of the warehouse. Andrew was tending to one of the boats.

He looked up at her for a moment and gave her a nod like he knew she wanted to talk, but it also signaled he would be a minute. He pulled the frame out of the raft, then tipped the boat on its side, propping it up with the oars so he could spray it off. Some of the water caught on the breeze and misted her. It felt good, and she stepped closer. Andrew noticed the movement and flicked the hose at her, showering her with the cold water.

"Hey!" She tried to sound indignant, but she didn't step away.

"I thought you wanted to get wet."

"What I'm about to do is going to get me wet—maybe too wet." She wiped the moisture from her arm. "I might be in over my head with this one."

Andrew gave her a knowing look. "I'll be there to bail you out if it gets too deep."

A funny surge shot through Kenedee's stomach, not at the idea of Andrew bailing her out but at the notion of being in over her head with Dravin. Maybe this wouldn't be such a bad thing—if it worked. If she helped save Dravin's business, there might be a significant shift between them. Hopefully a positive one. "If everything goes as planned, maybe I won't want to be bailed out."

Andrew turned away from the boat and looked at her. There was a tightness behind his eyes, and instantly, Kenedee regretted her words. She thought they were cryptic enough, but Andrew's brows had pulled down, darkening his expression. She had to be more careful. It didn't look good for her to be chasing after someone who currently had a girlfriend, no matter how obnoxious that girlfriend was. But even more than that, she didn't want Andrew to find out how much she liked his brother.

She lifted her head and tried to look innocent. "I'm ready when you are."

It was another twenty minutes before all the gear was washed off and they were alone in the warehouse. Andrew handed her a cheap-looking cell phone. "Prepaid," he explained, "so Dravin won't recognize the number. It might take several phone calls to work this deal out, but when you're done, you can toss the phone. It's not worth anything." Kenedee turned the phone over in her hand, looking at it as Andrew continued. "Keep this simple. You don't have to commit to booking the trips. Just tell him you're interested."

Kenedee wiped her brow nervously. She wasn't sure that would be enough to convince Dravin. "And two hundred employees? It sounds kind of . . . I don't know . . . fake."

"Make it two hundred twenty-six. It doesn't matter as long as it's up there."

Kenedee's fingers trembled as she dialed the number, and her mouth went dry when Dravin answered.

"Hi, um . . . this is Miss Kathy Hampton." She stumbled over the words, wondering if he could already detect the lie. Using her best accent, she went on to explain the imaginary company and her intent to send her employees on a river trip. Her breath caught in her throat as she finished the rehearsed lines. She waited, hoping he hadn't recognized her voice.

He hadn't. Dravin's response was exactly what she wanted. She could even detect the hope in his voice. It was good, and at the same time, it filled her with guilt. She paused, unable to go on. This was all fake, and she was giving him false hope.

Andrew nudged her, his eyebrows raised in concern, which made her feel all the more torn. She didn't want to let Andrew down either.

"Miss Hampton? Are you there?" Dravin's voice sounded from the other end.

Andrew nudged her again.

"That's right, Mr. Grant," she finally said, "two-hundred and twenty six."

"That's great!" Dravin's voice rose with excitement. "We'll be happy to accommodate you."

Out of the corner of her eye, she saw Andrew pumping his fist in the air. She scheduled some rough dates in August with Dravin and promised to call him back to finalize the details. By the time she pressed end on her phone, the hesitation she had felt before was gone. She liked making him happy.

She pocketed the phone and looked at Andrew. He was grinning. Like always, his expression grabbed her when he smiled. It was whimsical and sweet all at the same time, and she grinned back in response. He opened his arms to hug her, and she willingly stepped forward, but as soon as their arms touched, she saw Dravin. With a startled jerk, she pulled away.

Andrew looked disappointed for a moment, but then he turned and watched Dravin walk toward the warehouse.

"He must be coming to tell us the good news," Kenedee said. But Dravin suddenly stopped and pulled out his phone. The smile fell from her face. He was probably calling Charlotte.

"Looks like we'll have to wait a few minutes." Andrew walked over to the boat, which was still propped up on its side. It was nearly dry.

Kenedee followed him until the cell phone buzzed. She yanked it from her pocket, silencing it as she looked at the number. The blood drained from her face. "Dravin is calling back." She held the phone out for Andrew to see, then they both looked back at Dravin. He was turned away with his cell phone to his ear.

Andrew's eyes widened. "He's calling Kathy Hampton."

A jolt shot through Kenedee's stomach, and she stepped closer to Andrew. If Dravin turned around and saw her, it would all be over. The phone vibrated in her hand again just as Dravin started to turn.

Andrew was suddenly in motion. He pushed up on the boat they were standing next to, letting the oars that were supporting it drop to the ground. He wrapped his free arm around Kenedee and pulled her close to him. For a brief moment, she stiffened, then realized what he was doing. She willingly pressed herself against his chest just as he lowered the boat over them. He crouched over her, and they both dropped to the ground until they lay next to each other. His arm that was supporting the boat was now resting across her back, and the raft completely covered them.

Her phone buzzed again. "Answer it," he whispered.

It was a tight fit under the boat with Andrew so close to her, but she managed to move the phone up to her ear. "Hello?" Her voice sounded muffled and breathless in the close quarters.

"Miss Hampton, this is Dravin Grant again."

Kenedee turned her head. There was a natural gap under the edge of the boat, and she could see Dravin's gray Newport sandals in the distance. He appeared to be pacing back and forth. "Yes? What can I do for you?"

"I just wanted to ask how you heard about our company."

A prickle of sweat broke out on her forehead. "I . . . um . . . picked up one of your brochures."

"Oh?" Dravin's voice brightened. "We just put them out today, so you must be in town."

Kenedee cringed as she realized her mistake. "Just passing through."

"Well, I'd love to meet if you have a moment."

"No," Andrew whispered. His head was so close to hers that he could hear what Dravin was saying.

Kenedee's mind raced frantically. There were any number of excuses she could use to decline the meeting, but then she took a deep breath and said, "How about tomorrow night? Eight o'clock at your office?"

"Sounds great," Dravin said. "I'll see you then."

Kenedee pressed end on her phone, then turned her head to look at Andrew. It was too dark under the boat to make out his expression, though his face was only a few inches from hers. She lay quiet for a minute, feeling him next to her. His breath came heavy and ruffled the hair around her face. His arm was still across her back as she lay tucked against his side. "Say something," she finally said.

Andrew let out a long, slow breath, and she could smell the mint from his gum. "Well, that didn't go as I expected," he whispered. "Why didn't you agree to something easier, like inviting him to your company office to meet with your two hundred and twenty-six employees?"

"Very funny. Just trust me on this. It'll work out." Kenedee shifted under his arm. There really wasn't room to move with the raft pressing down on them, so she hadn't expected him to pull it away, but now that she had time to think about it, she wasn't sure this was the best situation to be in. "Can we get out from under here now?"

"Dravin is still out there."

She turned and looked through the gap at the edge of the raft. Dravin was walking toward the warehouse again. His Newport sandals moved to the opening of the bay doors and stopped.

"Andrew, you out here?"

Kenedee held her breath. Their hiding place was safe enough. The boats were left to dry upside down on the ground as often as they were propped up on the oars, so Dravin shouldn't suspect anything, but for some reason, he lingered in the doorway. With every second that ticked by, Kenedee noticed how close Andrew was to her. She could feel his side move each time he took a breath and could feel the muscles of his arm tense around her. It kind of felt good. She took a moment to enjoy it, then lightly bit the inside of her cheek in penitence. She should be thinking about Dravin, not Andrew. She gritted her teeth and longed to push away from him, longed to get away from her confusing feelings.

At last Dravin turned and walked toward the office. As soon as he disappeared, Kenedee shifted again. "Can we get out now?"

"Yeah, I think it's safe." Andrew pushed himself up, lifting the boat with him. When Kenedee crawled out, he let it drop back onto the ground.

She had barely stood when she noticed Jackson standing not ten feet away from them. A smirk crossed his face. "Whoa, I did not expect to see that." He scratched his head. "I had no idea you guys were dating."

Kenedee scowled at him. "We're not!"

Jackson's grin broadened. "Suuurrre. I suppose you were just inspecting the raft for leaks."

Kenedee looked at Andrew. She expected him to jump in and explain that there weren't any feelings between them, but he just looked at her, his eyes steady and solidly fixed on her. What was he doing mixing up her feelings like that? She didn't like being confused, and she knew the one thing that would sort it out. She tossed a look back at Andrew as she turned away. "See ya later. I'm going to talk to Dravin."

Chapter 4

Kenedee clamped her hands into fists and resisted the urge to look over her shoulder. She expected Andrew to follow her, but he didn't. Shouldn't he be concerned that she would tell Dravin what was going on—that she would give up the ruse? She threw the door open to the office, making the bell clank loudly.

Emma looked up at her. "I knew it would backfire. Dravin caught you when he walked out to the yard, didn't he?"

"No." Kenedee suddenly felt defensive. "Andrew dropped a raft over us, and it was a perfect hiding spot. It went just as planned. I'm even meeting Dravin tomorrow night." She paused. "Well, technically he'll be expecting Kathy Hampton, but Kathy and me—we're like the same person, and she's kind of excited to have this private meeting with Dravin."

Emma nodded, but her eyes narrowed into slits. "Brilliant. You got a date with Dravin, but doesn't that—I don't know—ruin everything else?"

"Not really. I can work it out." Her mind was already rushing to figure out how to fix it.

"Maybe I'm just pessimistic, but it sounds like you're about to stick a cherry bomb in the mix and blow your little scam to pieces." Emma pointed a finger at her. "Your whole plan is going to be exposed when Dravin sees it's you. All you managed to do is shorten Andrew's time frame for bringing in business. Instead of having a couple of weeks to save the company, you've limited him to twenty-four hours."

Kenedee tried to suppress the guilt gnawing at her. She hadn't just shortened Andrew's time frame, she'd obliterated it. But with a little bit of luck—well, maybe a lot of luck—it could still work out. She looked at the door. Andrew still hadn't come after her.

"What's wrong?" Emma asked. "You waiting for someone?"

"I thought Andrew would come in." She looked at the door again. Maybe she should have stayed and talked to him. She really didn't mean to ruin his plan, but it didn't mean she couldn't salvage it.

"I wouldn't count on him coming in. He's probably out there plotting how to murder you."

"I didn't ruin things. I have ideas on how to fix this." She wasn't about to admit that they weren't completely formed ideas, or practical ones, for that matter.

Emma tapped her fingers on the counter. "So, how was it? You know—being under the raft with him?"

Kenedee swallowed and averted her eyes. "Like being stuffed in a closet with him. Not much room to move."

Emma appeared amused. "Sounds exciting. Maybe I should go out and hide under a raft too. If I could pick someone to be so close to I couldn't move, I'd pick Jackson. You think he's up for that?"

Kenedee shrugged. "Probably. He's that type of guy. He saw Andrew and me climb out from our hiding spot. He thought we were dating."

Emma grinned. She pulled out a piece of paper from her back pocket, unfolded it, and pushed it toward Kenedee.

The words *Bonus . . . He's single* jumped out at her. She grabbed the paper, crumpled it up, and tossed it at the garbage can. It missed and landed on the floor two feet from its target.

For a brief moment, Kenedee remembered how it had felt when Andrew had pulled her close to him as he'd lowered the raft over them. Something had surged through her at their closeness. It was probably just being near someone so strong. Like any typical river guide, Andrew was muscular, his body hard and toned from working the oars as he directed countless rafts through the white waters of the Colorado river. If that was it, then those feelings were just superficial. She looked at the vase of daisies on her desk, then reached out and brushed a finger across one. The bright yellow center seemed so happy, almost reminding her of Andrew's smile and how it brightened her day, but she refused to let her thoughts go in that direction. Dravin had given her the bouquet, and he had to be struggling to sort out his thoughts between her and Charlotte. The least she could do was wait to see how that would play out before she let her feelings get tangled with someone else.

"Can you watch the desk for a few more minutes?" Kenedee asked. "I need to talk to Dravin."

Emma slumped over the counter. "Sure. I have nothing better to do than sit here and watch you self-implode."

Kenedee walked into Dravin's office just as his cell phone rang. He greeted her with a nod but held up a finger, indicating that he was going to take the call.

"Hi," he said into his phone.

Kenedee felt her jaw tighten. It was Charlotte—she could tell by the way Dravin answered. He was trying to sound nice, but there was a tight strain in his voice.

"I don't want to guess what you're doing. Why don't you just tell me?" There was a pause, and then he spoke again. "You're looking at rings?" His chest rose and fell as his breath grew more labored with exasperation. "Can we talk about this later? I have someone in my office; I'll call you back in a few minutes." He didn't wait for her reply but hung up and pocketed the phone without a word.

Part of Kenedee admired Dravin for his patience and for trying not to hurt Charlotte, but it was only a matter of time before he broke up with her, and Kenedee longed for that day to come sooner rather than later.

"So . . . " Dravin leaned back in his chair, clasping his hands behind his head. "Did you hear our good news?"

Kenedee shrugged, not sure how to respond.

"We just got a booking for two hundred twenty-six people."

"Two hundred twenty-six?" That number was starting to annoy her. It was two hundred twenty-six lies she was telling him, and she couldn't stand it. Tomorrow night he would learn the truth, and then what would happen? He would know she had feelings for him, but at the same time, he would learn there wasn't a company sending its employees rafting.

Kenedee sat down in one of the chairs positioned in front of Dravin's desk and rubbed her forehead. "About that . . ." She paused and looked at him. "I don't think it's going to happen."

Dravin's expression changed, moving from excitement to surprise and then settling on a glum, quizzical look. It tore at her to see him so quickly deflated.

"Why? Do you know something I don't?"

She nodded.

Dravin swore softly, then swiveled his chair around and gazed out the window. "I should have known it was too good to be true."

He picked up a framed picture on the edge of his desk and looked at it. It was a picture of the rafting trip when Dravin had announced he was going to open his own river-rafting company. Kenedee had been there. In fact, she was in the photo. She and Dravin, along with four other boaters, frozen in time, their mouths open, screaming in delight, clinging to the sides of the raft as it tipped into the rapid known as Little Niagara. Andrew was there too, at the oars, his never-ending grin spread across his face. Both he and Dravin had been guides for another company at the time, and it had been a coincidence that Kenedee had ended up on that trip with them. She had won the excursion from being caller ten on KZMU Radio. Andrew had been showing off that day, as guides often did—surfing the raft on hydraulic waves, popping it up, and even flipping it on purpose. Their group was up for the excitement, and they loved every minute of it.

Dravin looked at her as he set the picture down. "Good times, huh?"

She nodded again.

"So, you said this deal isn't going to go through. What do you know about it that I don't?"

Kenedee felt his eyes on her, and she dropped her gaze to the picture on his desk. He looked so happy in the photo, sitting next to her in the raft. The air suddenly vibrated with the sound of his cell phone. He took it out and looked at it, his expression pinched. It was Charlotte, Kenedee guessed. Dravin hit silence and tossed it on his desk.

"She can wait." He leveled his gaze back on Kenedee. "So tell me what you know."

Kenedee looked at his cell phone. He had just dismissed Charlotte in favor of talking to her. She couldn't ruin it by shattering all of his hopes with the first sentence out of her mouth. "Nothing really," she said as she fidgeted with a loose string on the hem of her shorts.

"Don't tell me that. You just insinuated that you knew something."

She glanced up at him. "It's just that John with Canyon Cliff Adventures called. He can't make the meeting this afternoon." She didn't mention the five grand. That piece of confidential information hadn't been meant for her ears, but most likely, Dravin already knew about it. "He wants you to call him and reschedule for Friday."

Dravin nodded thoughtfully, then leaned back in his chair. "All right. So I take it you know I've been thinking of selling River Quest to them."

"Yes, Andrew told me."

"Well, you should also know that if this deal goes through with Kathy Hampton and her two hundred twenty-six employees, I won't sell out. That will take a huge chunk out of my loan payment, and Andrew's been working on getting some business with some multilevel marketing companies. Between the two, it should cover the whole loan. After that, we'll have enough cash flow to squeeze by for the rest of this season."

"It'll work out." Kenedee stood. She couldn't bring herself to tell him the truth—that there was no Kathy Hampton. No two hundred twenty-six employees. But there was a Miss Kenedee Roberts, and she would do whatever she could to help Dravin.

She braced herself as she walked out, prepared to have Emma hit her with a barrage of questions, but Emma wasn't at the desk. Andrew was.

He was holding one of the daisies and twirling the stem between his fingers. "Nice flowers."

"Thanks." She eyed him carefully. Did he know Dravin had been bringing them to her? Andrew's mouth was pressed into a tight line, showing his displeasure. She plucked the flower from his hand and put it back in the vase with the others. "I didn't tell Dravin about our plan, if that's what you're worried about."

"It doesn't matter. He'll know by tomorrow night anyway. Isn't that right, Miss Kathy Hampton?"

Kenedee folded her arms across her chest. "All right. I made a mistake. I really do want to help, but right now, I don't have any brilliant ideas that will fix everything by tomorrow. Do you want me to call him back and tell him I can't make the meeting?"

Andrew looked hard at her. "First tell me why you were so willing to meet him in the first place."

"I don't know." She pulled out the prepaid cell phone. "I'll call him right now and cancel the meeting."

Andrew reached out and snatched the phone away. "Oh, no you don't. You're going to meet him tomorrow as planned."

Kenedee made a grab for the phone, but he kept it out of reach. "Why?"

"It's what you want, isn't it? To meet Dravin . . . privately?"

Kenedee groaned inwardly. Emma must have told him. "And you don't approve because he already has a girlfriend, right?"

Andrew's face grew hard. "In my experience, love triangles seldom work."

"Then relax, because I'm not asking for your approval." Kenedee motioned for him to get out of her chair. If he really cared about any of it, he would've seen that Charlotte wasn't good for Dravin and that their relationship was already falling apart. And if he cared, he would've noticed that someone else had been giving her flowers for weeks.

"No, you don't need my approval." Andrew stood and leaned over the desk toward her. "And that's why you are going to meet with Dravin tomorrow. Apparently, you only agreed to help me so you could get close to him. Since that was your plan all along, let's see how it turns out."

Chapter 5

Kenedee parked her car behind the warehouse and watched as the sun spilled its light over the red cliffs in the distance. She usually didn't go to work this early, but thoughts about how her meeting with Dravin would go that evening were making her restless. It seemed like an eternity before she heard another vehicle pull into the parking lot.

She waited a few seconds, then got out of her car and strode toward the office, hoping to find some paperwork to drown herself in. Dravin's car was parked in front. The bell tinkled as she entered, and Dravin jumped at the sound. He wasn't in his office like she'd expected but was standing next to her desk. His hands flew behind his back, but not before Kenedee saw the new vase of daisies he was trying to hide.

For a brief second, she thought about turning around and walking out to let him have his anonymity. She could say she had forgotten something in her car. But she just stood there. Things were coming to a head anyway, so why try to hide it anymore?

Dravin looked down at the floor, letting a piece of his dark hair fall over one eye. "I didn't know you would be coming in so early."

She took a step toward him. "You're holding flowers behind your back."

He raised his gaze to meet hers, then slowly brought the flowers out. The daisies weren't the traditional white variety but were colored red, yellow, blue, and orange. They were bright and cheerful. "You weren't supposed to see them yet." He sat the vase on her desk next to the bouquet he had given her yesterday. She loved the additional flowers, but any more and her desk would resemble a funeral home.

"They're beautiful."

Dravin took a step away as if to distance himself from the act of giving them to her. "You still weren't supposed to see me."

She waved a hand dismissively. "Dravin, I've known about the flowers for a long time."

"You have? How much do you know?"

"More than you think, but for the record, I think it's sweet."

A look of relief crossed his face. "Just don't tell anyone, all right? Especially Andrew. For right now, this needs to be our secret."

She completely understood. Andrew wasn't about to put his stamp of approval on a relationship between Dravin and her anyway. But this was still a big step. She wanted to walk over and take his hand and tell him that everything would work out, but it didn't feel right. Instead, she walked over and adjusted the vase. "I love the flowers, but why two days in a row?"

"I guess you're that special." He winked. "Plus, we're celebrating. The expedition with Kathy Hampton is saving the business."

Kenedee shifted uneasily. She hadn't decided how to handle that situation yet, and this wasn't the moment to crush his hopes. After a long minute of silence, she decided to direct the focus back to him. "What about you and Charlotte?"

Dravin's face darkened. "I suppose everyone's noticed how bad our relationship has been lately. But I don't want to hurt her."

Kenedee tried to bury the lump rising in her throat. What would he do—keep both her and Charlotte on strings like his own personal marionettes?

"You need to make some decisions here," she prodded.

He put his hands up defensively. "I will. It's just that my mind has been preoccupied with the business. As soon as we're in the black, I'll set everything right."

* * *

It was a new record. Kenedee had been at work for six hours and hadn't spoken to Dravin for five hours and forty-eight minutes. Surprisingly, she found it quite easy to avoid him. The bell tinkled as Emma entered the office. "What are you doing here? I thought you took the day off to go to the dentist."

"I'm done." Emma smiled, and only one side of her face rose while the other side hung limp and motionless.

Kenedee would have laughed, but her emotions were wound so tightly she didn't even crack a smile. "So you're done playing with the tooth fairy, and you thought you could come in and pick up a run? Hate to say it, but we already had a walk-in this morning, a group of five. Andrew took them out. I don't think we'll get any more this late in the day, but if you want to hang around—"

"I'm actually here to see you," Emma said with a slur. "Did you decide what you're going to do tonight?"

Kenedee stood and began to pace behind her desk. "You're the one who didn't want me to get involved in the first place, so I'm not sure I should fill you in on the drama."

"But it's the only exciting thing happening around here. Come on; just spill it."

"You already missed the excitement for the day." Kenedee picked up the new vase of flowers and shook it until the water sloshed out over her hand.

"Don't strangle them." Emma grabbed the vase and sat it back on the table. "Just tell me what happened."

"I caught Dravin putting them on my desk this morning." She pointed an accusatory finger at the brightly colored daisies.

"For real? You mean you walked in on him in the act?" Emma's half smile took on a new intensity. "What'd he say?"

"He wants to keep it a secret for now."

"Of course. What man doesn't want to keep his mistress a secret?"

"I'm not his mistress," Kenedee growled.

"Yeah, yeah. What else did he say?"

"Not much. He said he didn't want to hurt Charlotte and that he'll make things right when his mind isn't so focused on the business."

Emma's half smile turned into a half frown. "That's it? No declaration of love? No sonnets? No fireworks?"

Kenedee allowed her own disappointment to show in her expression. "If there were a class to teach men how to be romantic,

I know a couple of them who should sign up. And it's not that I expect sonnets or fireworks. But seriously, Dravin could've given me more than a passive excuse about waiting until the business is in the black. I mean, what am I? His loan officer? As if we can only be on good terms as long as there's a good cash flow?" Kenedee let out a long breath, and with it, a heaviness settled over her. She stared down at her feet and listened to her heart thumping dully in her chest.

"You want me to beat him up?" Emma asked.

"I don't think that will cheer me up. It's just that I expected things to change after he admitted to giving me the flowers. I thought things would move forward, but no."

"It feels like you're stuck in a stagnant pond of muddy water?"

Kenedee rubbed her forehead. Was this the beginning of another river analogy—something about water always flowing? She couldn't wrap her mind around it now. She needed to sort out her own mess of thoughts. She wasn't exactly sure why she was so disappointed in Dravin—or maybe she did know and just didn't want to admit it. Intruding thoughts of Andrew had been inundating her, and she'd hoped that once Dravin had admitted to the flowers—admitted to liking her—her uncertainty would disappear. But it hadn't worked out that way.

"You'll just have to do something about it," Emma said. "You don't have to wait for Dravin to make a move."

Kenedee snatched an orange daisy from the vase and began to twist the stem between her fingers. "I am doing something. I'm going to meet him tonight and sort things out."

"Take matters into your own hands. That's good, but isn't that a little problematic? I mean, who are you going to show up as? Kathy Hampton or Kenedee Roberts?"

"A little of both." Kenedee began plucking off the individual petals of the orange daisy in a he-loves-me, he-loves-me-not fashion. "Not only that—I'm going to get the business out of the red so Dravin can make some decisions. I'm not going to let him walk the fence. Once I know where his feelings lie, I can figure out my own."

"Sounds complicated, all except for that part about you getting the business out of the red. That ought to be simple enough. All you have to do is show up tonight with two hundred twenty-six employees ready to book a rafting trip."

"Yeah, simple . . ." Kenedee let her words trail off. "Actually, I've been on the phone all day with a Mr. Zackery. Just cross your fingers and pray that my deal with him works out."

"What deal?"

Kenedee stopped plucking petals and shook a finger at Emma. "I'm keeping it a secret for now, so in case it falls through, I won't look like a total idiot." Kenedee held up her orange daisy with the pedals missing. It looked half scalped.

"Like the crazy lady with the mutilated daisy would ever look like an idiot." Emma's face turned serious—at least half of it did. "Whatever you're planning, is it going to be enough to keep Dravin from selling to Canyon Cliff Adventures?"

"I hope so. But either way, selling or paying off the loan will take his mind off the problem. He should be able to *set things right.* I'm not a fish he can just keep on the line."

"So it all goes down at eight o'clock tonight." Emma looked at the clock. Kenedee didn't have to. It was five hours and twenty-five minutes away, and she was conscious of every second ticking toward it.

"Are you done making phone calls?" Emma asked.

"I'm calling Mr. Zackery at seven tonight to finalize things."

Half of Emma's face smiled again. "That gives you around four hours to relax." She held out her car keys. "I have my kayak loaded on top; life vest and paddle are on the backseat. I'll take over the desk for the rest of your shift. Go take a run down the daily stretch."

"Take the rest of the day off?" Kenedee looked at the proffered keys. "Well, I can't get in any more trouble than I'm already in, so why not?"

Chapter 6

The paddle moved with a harmonious cadence as each end dipped into the Colorado River. The flowing movement soothed Kenedee's emotions. She had chosen the eight-mile stretch just below the scenic Fisher Towers because it offered the perfect combination of mild rapids and peaceful stretches of water. Red sandstone cliffs towered on either side and melted away behind the green tamarisks that banked the river.

She had been on the water for about forty minutes when she spotted the twisted willow tree on the south side of the bank and directed the small red kayak toward it. Beneath the shade of the tree was a small clearing—her favorite stop along the river. It was secluded and slightly hidden, which made it the perfect place for sitting and reflecting on life's predicaments.

Kenedee nosed the kayak onto the sand bank just as a figure emerged from behind the tamarisks. Her heart fell. She would have to find somewhere else to be alone. She started pushing off again when the person came into full view. Her heart skipped a beat, and she stuck her paddle into the sand to keep the kayak from floating away. "What are you doing here?"

Andrew walked over and held his hand out to her. She hesitated but then took it. His grip was firm, and he easily pulled the kayak onto the bank.

"We passed you on the river road as we were taking our group back. I haven't had a chance to talk to you about tonight, so I dropped off the group and came back here."

Kenedee climbed out of the kayak and pulled it farther on shore so it wouldn't drift away. "But how did you know I'd stop here?"

The corners of his lips lifted, but the smile didn't quite form. He was still upset, and that shot a pang of disappointment through her.

"I know this is one of your favorite spots." He cocked his head to the side and looked at her. "And with everything that was going on, I thought you would stop here to scout your run."

Andrew's words weren't lost on Kenedee. She turned and looked out across the river. For the larger, more complicated rapids, boaters often beached their rafts and hiked up to scout the course before them, looking ahead to determine which path to take through the rough waters. This stretch of river didn't have any large rapids, so Andrew was clearly referring to the rough waters she would face tonight. She couldn't help but smile at his insight.

"You guessed right."

Andrew tossed his head, flipping his brown hair out of his eyes, but the breeze played with it for a second, then swept it back to where it was. She walked a few steps away and watched him. He seemed irritated. He kicked at the sand with the toe of his sandal, then picked up a small rock and hurled it across the water. It skipped several times, but he didn't watch it. Instead, he turned and walked toward her. His muscles were tense, and it showed as he folded his arms across his chest.

"I'm sorry," he said.

"About what?"

He turned his back to her and looked out across the water. Kenedee didn't say anything but watched as the breeze rippled his T-shirt across his shoulder blades.

"Look, Andrew, if you aren't going to talk to me, I'm going to get back on the river." Her own emotions were on a roller coaster, and she wasn't sure she could handle his inner torment on top of her own. She walked past him toward the kayak, but he reached out and put his hand on her shoulder. There was a quiet, determined strength in his fingers, not enough to hurt her but enough to make her pause.

"I'm sorry for pressuring you into meeting with Dravin." He let out a long sigh. "When Emma told me you had feelings for him . . ." His hand still rested on her shoulder, and she did nothing to remove it. She tried to read his expression, but he was trying so hard to control any emotion. Still, she thought she saw something. Frustration? Sadness?

"What are you trying to say?" she prompted.

"I don't know. I was mad. And not simply because Dravin has a girlfriend."

His hand slid from her shoulder, his fingers lightly touching her neck, and then softly he cupped her chin and lifted her head. A small jolt of excitement coursed through Kenedee, but Andrew's movement had been instinctual, and she saw the moment he realized it and dropped his hand.

She frowned at the loss of his touch and almost reached out to take his hand, but the same hesitation that bound him also bound her. Dravin stood between them. As long as Andrew thought she loved his brother, he would guard his own feelings. And until she settled things between Dravin and her, she would not risk Andrew's emotions. Maybe there was something starting between them, but they had to keep that barrier in place until things were sorted out. She would not flit between two relationships like Dravin did. Everything would have been so much simpler if Dravin had never given her flowers.

"So about tonight," Andrew said. "I don't want you to feel pressured into meeting with Dravin. In fact, I think it will be better if you call and cancel with him."

Kenedee studied his face. She didn't want to hurt Andrew, but she couldn't stand to be stuck between Dravin and him, unmoving, and tonight was her chance to change all that. And she did owe that much to Dravin. Perhaps it was simply because he had secretly lavished his attentions on her. Or maybe she just wanted to help him out of his bad relationship with Charlotte. Either way, she couldn't leave him hanging. "No, I'm not going to cancel."

Andrew's expression hardened, but the look in his eyes was more of regret than anything else. Whatever emotion he was feeling, he pushed it aside and tensed. "Why?" His voice was low, but he controlled the tone. "You still want to have your *date* with him? You don't care about the ramifications this has on the business as long as you grab his attention tonight?"

"It's not like that at all. And I've been working my own angle to help the business."

Surprise flashed across Andrew's face, and then it was gone. "I hope it works out for you. From what Emma said, it sounded like the only reason you were doing this was to get close to Dravin."

Kenedee felt her muscles tighten. She couldn't deny it because that was exactly why she had agreed to get involved. And that was why she had initially agreed to meet with Dravin. But that was before she had questioned her feelings—before Andrew had made her truly question her feelings.

Andrew reached up and pulled his hand down a willow branch, stripping the leaves from it. "If your intent is to help the business, then just cancel the meeting and give me a couple of days to get a contract with the companies I've been working with. You can still work out your own deal too."

"A couple of days won't help. Obviously Dravin hasn't told you that Canyon Cliff Adventures is offering an extra five grand and wants the sale expedited to this Friday."

Andrew's expression blanched. He shook his head and ran his fingers through his hair. "It doesn't matter. We can still work it out if we go back to the original plan. Dravin won't sell if he thinks the money is coming in from Kathy Hampton. The only thing that will ruin it is if you expose everything by showing up tonight."

Kenedee shook her head. She admired Andrew's determination, but realistically, they had till Friday to come up with the money, and she wouldn't risk misleading Dravin on false hopes past that deadline. "I'm sorry, but I can't—"

Andrew let out a groan. "You're still going to meet with him." A mournful expression crossed his face. "I think I understand. It's a lot harder to paddle upstream than it is to keep going in the same direction."

Kenedee opened her mouth to explain, but Andrew turned abruptly and walked away, crashing through the shrubs toward the road, where his jeep was parked.

Chapter 7

Kenedee leaned forward and nervously tapped her pen on her desk as she listened to Mr. Zackery. Whatever the cost, she had to make this deal go through, and she had to do it now.

"You do know the type of kids we deal with," Mr. Zackery said on the other end of the line. "We don't usually have any problems with violence, but pretty much all of them cop an attitude. They're more bark than bite, but their language can get pretty vulgar. Are you sure your river guides can handle that?"

"Of course." Kenedee adjusted the phone at her ear. "Personally, I know a few of our guides who will be excited to hear we're partnering with a wilderness camp for troubled youth. It might be a challenge working with the teens, but it will be rewarding too. And I think you'll see a change in the kids' attitudes while they're on the water. The river has a way of bringing people together, and it will put them in a situation where they'll want to work together." There was a pause on the end of the line as if Mr. Zackery was thinking.

"Well, you have me sold. I think this will be a valuable addition to our program."

Kenedee's heart leapt with excitement. She looked at the clock: seven twenty. She would be able to seal the deal before Dravin arrived. "And the price we discussed is fine with you?"

"I don't see why not. I've crunched the numbers, and with the added benefit it brings to our program, I think we can offset the cost."

Kenedee let out the breath she'd been holding. Everything was falling into place. "Great! So it's a go?"

"Just about. I have the e-mail you sent me with all the details, so I'll pitch it to the board at our next meeting."

Kenedee felt the breath go out of her like a balloon deflating. "Your next meeting?"

"Oh, don't worry. I love the idea of adding a rafting trip to our itinerary, and I'm sure the other board members will too. We'll have things approved by next month."

A month. That wouldn't help River Quest now. It wasn't going to work after all. Dravin *would* have to sell. She looked around the small office as reality set in. Within a week, all of this would belong to somebody else. She closed her eyes, and a single tear rolled down her cheek. She wouldn't be here. Even if Canyon Cliff Adventures kept some of River Quest's employees, she couldn't stand to work for the cardboard company with its canned adventures.

She looked at the clock again. Dravin would be arriving shortly to meet Miss Kathy Hampton. She ended the call with Mr. Zackery, then sat back in her chair and imagined what Dravin's expression would be when he learned the truth. She had planned to counteract his disappointment with her own solution to save the business, but none of that would happen now.

The sound of a car driving into the parking lot interrupted her thoughts. There were no more fantasies. Dravin was here, and she had to face the truth. She slumped in her chair and glanced down at her summer blouse and knee-length tiered skirt. It was just like her to overdress for an impending disaster. She thumped her head on her desk and bemoaned the fact that she had curled her hair for the occasion. The bell tinkled, and heavy footsteps moved toward her.

She braced herself, then looked up and gasped. "Emma! What are you doing here?"

"You didn't expect me to stay away, did you? Not with all the excitement going on."

"You can't be here when Dravin gets here."

"Don't worry. Jackson and I will hide in the warehouse."

Kenedee stood. "You brought Jackson with you?"

"We'll keep out of sight." Emma nodded her head toward the back of the building. "I parked my car on the back side so Dravin will never even know we're here."

"You need to leave, Emma. There isn't going to be anything exciting tonight."

Emma blinked several times and studied her face. "Wait a minute. Have you been crying?"

Kenedee threw her hands in the air. "Of course. I'm about to have my every wish come true. I have a date with Dravin. Why wouldn't I be crying?"

"The deal you were working on didn't go through, did it?"

Kenedee shook her head. "Not in time to make a difference." One more tear managed to squeeze its way out despite her attempt to hold it in.

"We can fix this." Emma dropped her purse on the counter and dug through it. She pulled out a candy bar but must not have been willing to part with it because she put it aside, then went back to digging in her purse. A second later, she extracted some face powder and a tube of lipstick.

Kenedee plopped down in her chair and protested as Emma went to work blotting and powdering. "Don't stress about it," Emma said. "You tried, and that's all that counts." Kenedee started to argue, but Emma silenced her with a coating of lipstick. "We'll get through it, even if we end up working for Canyon *Stiff* Adventures. You still need to salvage what you can of the evening."

Kenedee pulled away from her. "And how do I do that?"

"This is your one chance to be alone with Dravin. At the very least, you can see where that relationship is heading."

They looked at each other for a long moment, and Kenedee finally nodded, then jerked her head around and looked toward the window. The sound of a car engine broke the silence. "Oh no, he's here."

Emma gave her a thumbs-up. "Don't worry. You look great."

"I wasn't worried about my looks. I'm worried that Dravin is coming in here expecting to meet Kathy Hampton and he's going to find a River Quest employee party."

"No, he won't. Jackson is already hiding in the warehouse, and I'll slip out the back window right now. He won't suspect a thing."

Kenedee shook her head in dismay and followed Emma into Dravin's office to help her climb out the window. It went as well as expected. Emma punched out the screen with the promise to replace it and then snagged her pants as she climbed out, tearing a large hole in them.

Kenedee hurried back to her desk and sat down just as the bell tinkled. She looked up to greet Dravin. Words of her excuse formed in her mind and then suddenly evaporated. "Andrew?" She slapped a hand to her forehead. "This can't be happening. This really is a River Quest employee party."

Andrew glanced around at the empty room, then turned back on her. "I have to say, you wear the party look well." He still wore the thin, faded T-shirt and his cargo shorts he'd had on earlier.

"What are you doing here, Andrew?" She tried not to sound uneasy, but it didn't work. She couldn't help it. She didn't want him to be here, not when she was trying to sort things out with Dravin, who would be arriving any minute. Ugh. She liked that shirt on Andrew. She pinched her eyes shut for a moment and mentally scolded herself.

Andrew held up a thick, bulging envelope. "I'm not going to let you take all the heat when you tell Dravin the truth."

"What is that?" She eyed the envelope.

"It's money." He handed it to her, and she thumbed through it. It was full of hundred-dollar bills—a lot of them.

"And what do you want me to do with it?"

"It's for Dravin's loan. I've been saving for a Harley for a couple years now. There's thirteen thousand there." He nodded toward the envelope. "That will cover about half of the payment. Dravin can sell the company jeep, and that should get him close enough."

Kenedee looked at the pile of money. "Are you going to explain this to Dravin when he gets here?"

"No. I'm going to leave before he arrives. I want *you* to explain it. But more importantly, I want you to claim it. Say the money is yours, or tell him you worked out a deal with another company to get it. I don't care as long as he thinks it came from you."

Kenedee shoved the envelope toward him, thumping it against his chest. "I can't do that."

He gently pushed her hand away. "I got you into this by asking you to scam Dravin. He'll be more forgiving of your part in it when you give him this money."

"Why are you doing this?"

His eyes looked tormented for a moment. "Dravin doesn't talk to me about his relationships, but from what Emma said . . ." The muscles in his jaw tightened, and he started again. "If you and Dravin both care for each other, I don't want my scheme to mess things up between you two."

Kenedee looked at the two bouquets of flowers sitting on her desk. A week ago, those words would have sent a thrill through her, but right now, they settled on her like lead vapor, heavy and suffocating.

"But I'm not sure that's what I want," Kenedee said.

Andrew put his finger to her lips and hushed her. "Do you hear that?" She swallowed her words at his touch. Andrew cocked his head and looked at the door to Dravin's office. The sound of a window sliding open reached her ears, but she couldn't stop her mind from thinking about Andrew's finger still gently resting against her mouth.

Andrew tensed, then stepped in front of her, protectively. "Someone's breaking in."

Kenedee reluctantly focused back on reality. "That would be Emma and Jackson. My guess is they figured out that the warehouse isn't an ideal place to spy from."

Andrew looked at her for a moment, then slowly relaxed. "Why am I not surprised?" The sound of another car pulling into the parking lot drew their attention. This one *had* to be Dravin.

Andrew looked at the clock. "He's early. I thought the meeting wasn't until eight."

"It's only natural he'd arrive a little early." Kenedee held up the envelope of money. "I'm not going to give this to him. It's your money. If you want him to have it, *you* have to give it to him."

"Not if I'm not here." Andrew put a hand on the reception counter and bounded over it, landing in the space between the counter and her desk. He squatted down and disappeared.

"This isn't happening." Kenedee dropped the money and dashed around the counter. "You can't hide here." She pulled on his arm, trying to get him up.

"I've got to go somewhere, and it's not going to be in Dravin's office with the James Bond wannabes."

Unable to make him budge, Kenedee let go and held her hands out. "I can't do this with three people hiding and listening in."

The tormented look returned to Andrew's eyes. "I don't want to be here any more than you want me here. Take Dravin outside and have your conversation there."

Kenedee took a deep breath, trying to ward off the headache forming behind her eyes. Somehow, this wasn't how she imagined her *private* meeting. She let out a long breath and braced herself as she waited for the door to open.

Chapter 8

The bell tinkled, and Kenedee walked around the counter. Dravin stood in the doorway looking like he'd just stepped off the page of a sultry cologne ad—dark slacks, a dress shirt with the sleeves rolled to the elbows, and a loose, open tie. She wondered if he planned on tightening it when Kathy Hampton arrived.

He stared at her, stunned for a moment. "This is a pleasant surprise. What are you doing here so late?"

Kenedee waited for him to walk farther into the room, but he stood at the door, distracted, as if he really didn't care if she answered. Perhaps he was just anticipating Kathy's arrival.

He shot a quick glance toward Kenedee. "I didn't expect you to be here. I mean, you *can* be here. It's just that . . ." He looked back through the glass door.

"She's not coming." Just as Kenedee spoke the words, Dravin opened the door.

"She's here," he said.

Kenedee's mouth fell open as she watched a woman walk in. She wore a slimming, coral-pink cocktail dress with lace cap sleeves. Between the short skirt and the plunging neckline, there was scarcely a yard of material, but the whole Vera Wang style looked pricey.

"Charlotte?" Kenedee gasped. "You brought Charlotte to our meeting?"

Dravin raised a brow. "What do you mean by *our meeting*? I'm supposed to be meeting Kathy Hampton."

Charlotte sidled up next to Dravin and slipped her arm around him as if she were laying claim to him. Kenedee put her hands on her hips and straightened her shoulders. "There is no Kathy Hampton."

"What are you talking about?" Dravin said with a smirk.

"There is no Kathy Hampton." There was a surge of relief that came with admitting the truth. "It was me on the phone, trying to get you not to sell to Canyon Cliff Adventures."

Dravin's expression turned serious and then darkened with disappointment. "Really? I can't believe this. I'd expect something like this from Andrew . . . but not from you."

Kenedee took a step back so she could see Andrew and shot him a warning look to stay put.

It didn't work. Andrew stood and faced his brother. "It was my idea, Dravin."

Kenedee rolled her eyes. "Welcome to the River Quest employee party," she mumbled.

Dravin threw his hands in the air. "This totally makes sense now. What were you trying to do, Andrew? Get me to default on the loan? Because that's what would have happened if you would've kept playing it up."

Andrew grabbed the money envelope and tossed it at Dravin. "No, I wasn't, and whatever you think, don't blame Kenedee. It isn't her fault."

"What's this?" Dravin looked in the envelope.

"Thirteen grand to go toward the loan."

"That's thoughtful of you." Dravin thumbed through the money. "It almost makes up for the whole Kathy Hampton trick." He tossed the envelope back to Andrew. "But you can keep your money."

Andrew's posture grew rigid. "I know it's not enough to cover the loan, but we can still work it out. We can sell the jeep, or we can—"

"It's too late," Dravin cut in. "There is no loan. The payment's been made."

Andrew's jaw clenched, and Kenedee could feel his frustration building. "You already sold to Canyon Cliff Adventures?"

"No. You think I'd just sell River Quest without a fight? I mean we got an investor."

"Who?"

Charlotte pretended to examine a fingernail. "Who do you think?" She flipped her long blonde hair to the side. "Daddy left me an inheritance."

Kenedee's mouth fell open. She couldn't bring herself to say anything, but Andrew stepped forward, glaring at his brother. "Now I understand. That's why you wouldn't let Charlotte go while you were . . . intrigued with another woman." He glanced at Kenedee.

Charlotte gasped and rounded on Dravin. "There's another woman?" Her voice rose to a high pitch. "Who is it?"

"Kenedee," Andrew said in a growl. "And I won't let you toy with her like this."

Kenedee's insides were twisting now. She put a hand on Andrew's arm, but he shook it off. The air vibrated with the growing tension. Kenedee could feel Andrew's frustration wrapping around him like a spring. She stepped in front of him and put both hands on his chest. "Stop. You don't need to do this."

Dravin backed up, his face etched with uncertainty. "What are you talking about?"

Kenedee groaned. How could he pretend like he didn't know what was going on? In a minute, he would probably deny everything, but that didn't matter. She had made her own decision. "He was talking about us, Dravin—you and me."

Charlotte put a hand up. "Excuse me? Dravin is taken. So whatever fantasy is going through your head, forget it. He's mine."

"Yes, he is." Kenedee's voice dropped apologetically. "I made a mistake."

"It's not your mistake," Andrew said. "Dravin's the one—"

Kenedee put a finger against Andrew's lips to quiet him. It worked, and he calmed down at her touch. "I was the one in the wrong," she said. "I allowed my feelings to grow for Dravin when I shouldn't have. I really don't want to be with him after all. It's just that I felt obligated because he kept bringing me flowers."

Charlotte shoved Dravin. "How could you?" She spun around and jerked the door open, clanking the bell, then stormed out in a huff. Dravin stared after her, stunned.

Andrew looked down at Kenedee, searching her face. "All this is about the flowers?"

"What was I supposed to feel? Dravin has been giving me flowers for over a month now. I wasn't looking to fall in love with him, but the flowers kept coming, and he didn't seem like he was very happy with Charlotte—"

Dravin started chuckling. It wasn't a this-is-funny laugh but an I-can't-believe-this-is-happening laugh. "I take it you've got things from here?" A look passed between Andrew and him. It was a bit of regret mixed with frustration, but there was something else—an unspoken understanding that seemed to mark things as settled. Then a small smile played at the edges of Dravin's mouth, and he turned and ran after Charlotte. She hadn't gone very far. She seemed to like the drama and had lingered only ten feet from the door.

Kenedee dropped her head. She really hadn't meant to hurt Charlotte. She pinched her eyes shut and fought the emotion building there. A moment later, she felt Andrew's hands on her shoulders.

"The flowers were mine, Kenedee."

She jerked her head up and stared at him. "What?"

"I'm the one who gave you the flowers. Dravin just delivered them for me."

Kenedee leaned back, her eyes wide. All this time it was him? She thought back to when she had caught Dravin with the flowers yesterday. That was what he'd meant when he'd told her not to tell Andrew: he was trying to keep *Andrew's* secret.

Andrew shifted back and forth on his feet. "I thought you had figured it out. I've liked you ever since we met. I thought you knew that when you went on that first river trip with Dravin and me."

Kenedee recalled how Andrew had played everything up by showing off. She began pacing back and forth, her mind finally making sense of everything.

"Are you mad at me?" he asked. He reached out and put a hand on her arm, stopping her.

She pulled away. "Yes, I am mad!"

He caught her hand and gently held it. "Mad that it wasn't Dravin giving you the flowers?"

"No, I'm mad that you never told me you had feelings for me. Here I've been falling for you and wrestling with guilt because I thought *Dravin* was the one giving me flowers. And it was you all along? My heart's wanted to go one direction, and I've been trying to force it somewhere else, and all this time . . . it was you. Why didn't you ever say the flowers were from you?"

Andrew put his hand under her chin and raised it until she had to look at him. He searched her face for a moment. "That's what you're upset about?"

"Yes. Why keep it a secret when you thought I had already figured it out?"

He shrugged. "I thought it would be fun—you know, the whole secret-admirer thing. And Dravin was always the first one here in the mornings, so I thought he'd never get caught." He smirked. "Now that I think about it, it was a dumb idea. Is there any way I can make it up to you?"

"No more secrets. Just be straightforward with me."

He searched her eyes. "Are you sure you want that?"

She nodded, and he instantly slid his arms around her and pulled her close to him. "Is this forward enough?"

Kenedee could hardly catch her breath, but she nodded her head.

The bell tinkled as Dravin walked in again. Another look passed between the brothers, one that said everything was going to be okay now.

Kenedee offered Dravin an apologetic look. "I'm sorry about that. How's Charlotte?"

He gestured to where Charlotte stood by the car. "I explained everything to her, but she still wants me to fire you."

"I can't blame you if you do—"

He shook his head. "It's not going to happen. I'll pacify Charlotte by taking her ring shopping. I've always intended to, but I've never gotten around to it. Been too stressed about the business." He looked out the door again. "I guess I've really been neglecting her. That's why I came back in. I'm taking Charlotte out for a nice dinner and a movie. Give me one of those Ben Franklins." He held his hand out to Andrew. "You owe me at least that much."

"Come on," Andrew complained, but at the same time, he opened the envelope and pulled out one of the bills. "After all I've done to help you with the business, and now you're bumming money off of me?"

"Yep." Dravin didn't look remorseful in the least. "And I still expect you to come through with some of those companies you've been working with."

"No way. Now that the loan is paid off, I'm going to spend my time on the river."

"Remember who the boss is. Besides, we still need to build our customer base, so you can work the phones to get your deals to go through, and I'll take a few runs."

"All right," Kenedee said. "How about you both take a few runs. As for building our customer base, a Mr. Zackery will be calling in a few weeks. He wants to partner with River Quest to add a rafting trip to his wilderness treks for troubled youth."

Andrew looked at her and gave her another grin, one that said how impressed he was.

"You aren't the only one who can work deals," she said.

Andrew leaned down and, without warning, covered her mouth with a firm kiss. Kenedee gasped, but she didn't pull away. After a moment, Andrew softened his touch, and she let the warm sensation flow through her. Her lips lingered on his, and her emotions swirling together, clearing her mind of any confusion. It was Andrew who filled every crevice of her thoughts now, and that was exactly how she wanted it.

The door to Dravin's office opened, and Emma's voice sounded from the room. "Can we come out now?"

Kenedee reluctantly pulled away from Andrew and looked around.

Dravin rolled his eyes as Emma and Jackson emerged from his office. "What are you doing in there—" He held a hand up. "Never mind. Don't tell me. I don't want to know. I'm leaving now." He turned and then paused. "Canyon Cliff Adventures would've backed out of the sale once they knew what a nuthouse they were getting." He looked over his shoulder, winked, then walked out.

"See." Jackson playfully elbowed Emma in the ribs. "See, I told you they were a couple."

Emma pulled a crumpled piece of paper from her purse, opened it, and smoothed it out. At last she turned it around for everyone to see. The words *Bonus . . . He's single* were still legible, and the arrow was pointed directly at Andrew.

Kenedee wrapped her arms around Andrew's neck again and waited for his smile. She didn't have to wait long. When a grin broke across his face, she pulled him close and rose up on her toes, pressing her lips firmly against his.

When Kenedee broke away, Emma was bouncing up and down and strutting around as if she had just made a touchdown in the Super Bowl. She waved the paper in the air until Kenedee snatched it away.

"Your paper's wrong this time." She wadded the paper into a ball and lobbed it at the trash can. It hit its mark, but Kenedee was too preoccupied to notice. She intertwined her fingers with Andrew's and pulled him close again. "I don't think he's single anymore."

OTHER BOOKS AND AUDIO BOOKS
BY JENNIFER K. CLARK

Mark of Royalty (coauthored with Stephonie K. Williams)

The Knight of Redmond

Bonds of Loyalty

Fools of Us All

by
JULIE DAINES

To Paul and Mason and the whole film crew.
Thanks! Best experience ever.

Chapter 1

"Jennica?" a voice said from behind me. A man's voice I didn't recognize.

I pulled my shopping cart closer and kept my eyes on the cereal box's nutrition label. Eleven grams of sugar. I waited for him to realize his mistake and walk away. The soft tap of retreating footsteps did not reach my ears. Funny how the absence of a sound only made it louder. Whoever he was, he was still there.

I was not Jennica.

I understood his confusion. Jennica and I had the exact same hair—not quite red but not auburn either, wavy on the best day, frizzy on the worst. Same short, wiry build.

Mistaken identity had happened all the time back when I lived in Cedar Springs. But since I'd moved to the city, this was a first.

If I ignored him long enough, hopefully he'd go away. Then I wouldn't have to fake smile, offer up some idle chitchat, and pretend to laugh about how identical I am to my identical twin sister.

He put a hand on my shoulder and turned me. "Jennica. Hi. Long time no see."

First of all, why was he touching me? And second, anyone who led off with "long time no see" was automatically inducted into my Annoying People Hall of Fame. I lowered the cereal box and looked up, smile fixed, ready to explain. "I'm not—Mason?"

"Hey! You remembered me." He laughed, and his blue eyes twinkled. "Sheesh, Jen. I haven't seen you since high school. That was like, what? Eight years ago? You look great."

Must have been all that sitting around watching TV. I put the box of Crunchberries in my shopping cart to conceal the pack of Depends.

Mason MacIntyre. I'd had the biggest crush on him in high school—along with every other female in the school district. He moved in just in time for his senior year. My sister and I were juniors. He never knew I existed, even though he went out with Jennica for a couple months until she dumped him for some college guy.

Now Mason stood before me spouting one-liners and looking dreamy as ever.

"When did you move to the city? I thought you were off to LA to make it big or something," he said.

That was definitely my sister. The minute she had her high school diploma, she took off to be the next cover of *People* magazine. She'd probably make it too, knowing Jennica.

By default, I'd been the one to stay behind. I'd taken my aspirations of being an English teacher to the community college—up until the accident. Then I shifted all my classes to online and watched daytime television with my mother. Or, more specifically, I watched my mother watch daytime television.

He checked his watch. "Jen, I'm so sorry to rush. I'm late for something. I've got to run. But I'd love to see you again and catch up. Are you free for dinner tomorrow night?"

"Um. Yeah, I guess." Which I shouldn't have said because I wasn't Jennica. I was Jane. I didn't even get the good name. But I had a hard time caring about technicalities when my dreams were coming true all these years too late.

He grabbed my hand that had been gripping the shopping cart handle and squeezed it. "Great! Meet me at Red Marlin at eight."

I watched his dark head hurry around the corner toward the checkout lines.

He was gone.

What just happened?

At the tail end of twenty-six, I considered myself an adult, but the moment I had looked into Mason's eyes, I was seventeen again. I put the Crunchberries back on the shelf and grabbed a nice, responsible box of granola. Feeling weak in the knees or light-headed because an old crush asked me out was cliché. I hated clichés. And I hated seafood. And I really hated being mistaken for Jennica, but that was even more common than clichés.

Forget the clichés. What concerned me was the irony. He seemed genuinely excited about dinner with a girl who had dumped him his senior year—and I wasn't even that girl.

I'd spent years trying to be her. Oh heavens, how I'd tried. I'd talked like her, dressed like her, listened to the music she liked, gone where she'd gone, done what she'd done. Jennica was the only family member who escaped my father's temper. I'd thought if I could just be like her, I would avoid it too.

By the time I reached junior high, I realized it didn't work that way. There was no escape.

When the stress of trying to be someone else finally caught up with me, I missed a week of seventh grade due to a bad case of hives. Mom said it was probably an allergic reaction. I told her it was an outward expression of my inward affliction.

"Don't overanalyze everything, Jane," she'd said.

That's what she always said. I just never quite figured out how to do it.

Chapter 2

"Here's your lunch, Mom." I set a plate on her wheelchair tray. "Chicken salad. Your favorite."

"Thank you." She placed her napkin in her lap. "Do you need a ride to cheerleading?"

She remembered her manners perfectly well but not which daughter fed her, bathed her, and sat with her day in and day out. "Mom, it's me. Jane."

"Oh, Jane! How was school?"

I twisted the lid off her protein shake. "Fine." Not everything was worth correcting. It would be forgotten the next minute anyway. "I met this guy I used to like. Jennica's old boyfriend. Mason? Remember him?"

Jennica never brought her guys around the house, but Mason had come over once to surprise her. She'd made an abbreviated introduction to my mom—Dad wasn't home, thank goodness—then hauled him out the door before he could see me peeking from around the corner.

"He asked me out, even though he thinks I'm her. So there's that," I told Mom.

She chewed her sandwich, dabbing at the corners of her mouth with her napkin, her eyes glazed as she stared at the soap opera.

What I wouldn't give for an answer—a real answer. Mom had married young. Too young. And Jennica and I had come along less than a year later. She was barely into the second half of her forties now, but with her wheelchair, easy-care clothing, and weary face, she looked much older. We used to talk about everything. She was the only place in our family where I felt safe. She was my best friend.

Even now, I loved my time with her. But sometimes I wished for a little more lucidity in my conversation partner. It would be nice to be listened to *and* understood.

"He wants me to have dinner with him tomorrow night at Red Marlin. I know, I know. I don't like seafood. But I didn't have much of a say."

The TV remote slipped off the arm of her wheelchair. I put it on her food tray, where she could reach it. "I suppose I should just be a no-show because I'm the wrong sister and all that, but . . . is it bad that I really want to go?"

She slurped her protein shake through the straw.

"The whole thing is ridiculous. Does he even know Jen has a twin sister? And what will he think of me when he finds out I'm not her?" I pulled Mom's blanket up over her legs. When the sun climbed out of the living room window, she always got cold. "I guess we'll find out when I tell him tomorrow night. Eight o'clock."

* * *

Millie knocked on the door and bustled in for her regular Friday night of babysitting. Her gray hair frizzed in every direction, and she wore a Hawaiian-print muumuu. I'd never seen her in anything else. When the temperature dropped, she put stretch pants on underneath.

She went straight to the living room and changed the channel. "I'm not sitting here all night watching that. Jeopardy's on."

I grabbed my keys. If I didn't hurry, I'd be late for dinner with Mason. "Thanks, Millie."

"Sure, sure. Have fun at the library."

Millie thought I went to the library every Friday night. Usually, I did. But not always. Occasionally, I went to a movie or out to eat . . . alone and too ashamed to admit it, even to my mother's babysitter, who spent her Friday nights watching TV with someone who didn't even know her name, so weren't we a pathetic pair.

I backed out of the driveway and drove through the neighborhood streets. I'd meet Mason for dinner, explain that I was Jane, not Jennica, we'd laugh, I'd refrain from commenting on the smell of fish, we'd shake hands, and then we'd part ways—after the meal, of course. I hadn't put mascara on for nothing.

He might think I'd tricked him on purpose, which I hadn't. I'd tried to tell him who I wasn't, but all that had come out was who he was. Then he'd run off, leaving his dinner invitation floating in the air.

How angry would he be? He'd seemed like a sensible guy in high school, which was saying something. In the eight years since then, his sensibleness would only have grown. At least I hoped. Did I want to eat dinner with a guy who was less sensible now than when he was in high school?

Don't overanalyze everything. If it didn't work out, I could still catch a late show.

I aimed my keys at the car and beeped the locks. A red swordfish smiled down at me over the entrance, welcoming me to Red Marlin.

"Hello, there," I said to the fish just to be friendly while I pulled open the door. "Wish me luck."

"Good luck, Jennica." Mason stuck out a long and muscular arm to prop the door open as I walked in.

I hadn't expected him to be in the vestibule. "Oh, um. I wasn't talking to you," I said, which implied I was talking to myself, which I wasn't. I hated accidental implications. "I was talking to the fish," I explained, as if that sounded better.

He glanced at a tank of death-row lobsters, rubber bands around their claws so they wouldn't self-destruct. I shook my head and pointed to the genial swordfish glowing neon red above the door. I'd only been on this date thirty seconds and already I'd learned a valuable lesson: I needed to get out more. I needed interaction with people who interacted back. Talking to my mother was not the same thing as talking to a guy who actually comprehended.

He laughed. "You always were a bit goofy."

Jennica was the opposite of goofy. She had a cold, calculated determination that catapulted her to the top of the popularity lists, where she ruled with fear and intimidation. Everyone knew her, and then they'd meet me: I didn't know you had a sister!

The waitress seated us at a quiet booth on the side wall. We ordered drinks. Water for me, the cheapest drink on the menu.

Mason smiled at me as he unrolled the silverware from his napkin. "It's great to see you again. How have you been?"

"We've been okay." I spoke of myself and my sister in the collective. I suppose it gave my answer some semblance of truth. I rarely heard from Jennica. I assumed if she wasn't okay, she would make contact.

The waitress came to take our order.

"I'll have the Mango Shrimp Salad, hold the shrimp," I said.

"No shrimp. Got it." She turned to Mason. He ordered salmon.

The waitress snapped her pad closed and left.

"I was really surprised to see you," Mason said. "Do you live here now?"

"Yes," I answered, but it felt wrong. The whole thing felt wrong. Maybe planning to tell him I was Jane after dinner was a bad idea. I needed to just open my mouth and explain the misunderstanding. Jennica and I looked exactly alike. It could happen to anyone.

I played it out in my mind. I would tell Mason there had been a mistake and that I was Jennica's sister, Jane. His face would turn to stone. Eyes wolfish yellow. He'd douse me with his cup of soda and stomp away. If I was lucky, I would escape the cheek slap.

"What's the matter?" he asked.

I looked up at him. "What?"

He pointed to my hands. I'd been fiddling with them, twisting and squeezing my left thumb with my right hand like maybe I could milk something out of it. "You always do that when something's bothering you."

Did I? I mean, I knew I did, but I'd never noticed Jennica did it too. I slipped my hands under the table.

Mason took a long sip of his drink, then dug into the crab cakes appetizer he'd ordered. "So tell me, how's life treating you?"

"Well," I said. "If you really want to know. About five years ago, my parents were in a car accident. My dad didn't make it, and my mom . . . She's never been the same since. So I came home from school to help her out. We couldn't afford to keep the big house in Cedar Springs, so we moved here."

He set his fork down and reached across the table, putting his giant, warm hands on mine—which had somehow found their way back onto the table. He looked right into my eyes. "I'm so sorry. I never knew. That must have been awful."

The din of random conversations and background music faded. I nodded. Even though I'd been living with the aftermath of the accident every day since, it was still hard to talk about, especially to someone who seemed like they sincerely cared.

The waitress came with our food and set the plates down in front of us. "Salmon." Clunk. "Mango shrimp salad minus the shrimp." Clunk. It was the biggest salad I'd ever seen. "Anything else?"

"No," Mason and I said in unison.

After the waitress walked away, Mason asked, "Are you working?"

"I work from home." I told him about my job doing copyedits for several companies needing help with their technical manuals and such. He listened and asked questions as though it was the most interesting task on the planet.

I explained my long-term goal to get a PhD in English.

He looked shocked. "I never pegged you for English. Or a PhD."

He meant Jennica, of course. But I was still curious. "Why?"

"You seem so different." He shrugged.

We'd been talking for a long time. Or, more accurately, I'd been talking, and he'd been listening. Listening and grinning at me with his twinkly blue eyes.

"Different how?" I asked.

He shrugged again. "It's hard to explain, but at the same time so obvious." He stirred the food on his plate with his fork. "Smarter. More . . . laid-back."

I raised my eyebrows at him. Ouch. If he had really been describing a former me, that would have stung.

"Not that you weren't smart before," he quickly added. "But now, I don't know. You sound wise." He laughed. "The old Jennica never talked like this."

He shifted uncomfortably in his seat, and I didn't want to press him. I already knew exactly what he meant. Jennica had some qualities, but she had issues too. Her temper constantly simmered on the verge of boiling point. Turn up the heat one tiny notch and you'd better run for cover.

Mason was thinking the same thing. I could see it in the way he watched me, his expression one of skeptical surprise. His five o'clock shadow balanced out his dark hair and eyebrows. When he smiled, his mouth lifted in a way that made his entire face look happy.

The dispensing of information had been far too one-sided. All this talk about the old Jennica had stalled the conversation. It was time for Mason to cough up some answers.

"What brings you to the city?" I asked.

He chuckled again, and I had to concentrate hard to swallow my food. "Enough about you; let's talk about me?"

"Exactly," I said.

"I'm doing my residency at Saint Mark's Hospital."

"A doctor?" Mr. Hot Football Player, Popular Man Extraordinaire, a doctor? He *had* grown up since high school. As I recalled, he and Jennica had cut every other class until his grade point average had fallen so low he'd nearly been disqualified from the team.

"Why so surprised?" he asked.

"I just . . . I never pictured you as the studious type."

"Can't judge a book by its cover. I suppose we're both not the same people we used to be."

He had that right. Me especially—and quite literally. In truth, I'd never spoken to Mason before yesterday in the grocery store. He was the kind of guy a girl like me worshiped from afar. I had it on good authority that Jennica had never mentioned me at all. She'd made a point of telling me she'd done her best to keep my entire existence a secret from her friends. Not an easy task considering we'd gone to the same school. When Jennica put her mind to something, she got what she wanted.

I reminded myself again that high school was a long time ago. I needed to move on. But it seemed like my life had stopped moving the moment my parents had crashed their car. I wallowed, trapped and stagnant, unable to crawl out of the mire, while Mason and Jennica and probably all the others were moving ahead and making something of their lives.

"What kind of doctor?" I asked.

"Emergency medicine." He ate the last of his food and pushed his plate away. "I feel like it's where I can do the most good. I've seen a lot of scared people come through the ER, and half the time, I think all they really need is to feel like someone cares. Plus, it makes me look like a hero." He grinned, and it did make him look heroic. "They come in sick, in pain. I patch them up and send them on to other doctors and specialists. But somehow, I always get the credit for saving them."

Why had my sister ever let him go? He seemed near perfect to me.

I leaned away from the table, telling myself to slow down. Way down.

I knew better than anybody that first impressions could be deceiving. One minute a guy is handsome, charming, and sweet, making friends with the whole world. Then put him behind closed doors and let his anger flare, and out pops the Big Bad Wolf, and he devours you whole. That was what happened to my mom, and the whole family had paid the price. I wouldn't let that happen to me.

The waitress showed up with the check. Mason paid with cash. I asked for a box so I could take home my leftover salad. The waitress got one from the serving station, and I scooped the leftovers into the Styrofoam container and folded it closed.

Mason walked me out. I looked back to say good-bye to the red swordfish above the entrance. I didn't see Mason stop, and when I turned back, I rammed into him, popping the takeout container open and spilling salad all down his front.

"Oh my gosh! I am so sorry." I put my arms up to shield myself. I'd done it now, and any second I'd feel his anger on the side of my face.

"It's okay," he said.

"I'm sorry. It was an accident. I'm so sorry." I sidestepped around him, clearing an escape path in case I needed to run.

"It's fine. It's only a little salad." He brushed it off.

I lowered my arms and straightened up. The dressing had left a grease stain on his shirt.

He stared at me for a long time.

My dad had been gone for five years, yet, still, he had a choke hold around my neck. "I can't believe I spilled on you." I was wringing my hands again. I put them behind my back, where they could do their worrying in private.

He took a step closer, his eyes steady on me, watching me with a look I didn't know how to categorize.

I backed away. How could I ever consider getting close to him? I'd lied to him. He thought I was my sister. This had been an amazing night, but it had to end. I didn't have time for a relationship in my life. And I didn't have the nerve. Charming and sweet couldn't last forever.

"Mason, thanks for the dinner. I'd better be going." I tossed my smashed salad container into a garbage can and hurried to my car.

"Wait." He followed me, putting a hand on the driver's-side door so I couldn't open it. "Maybe . . . we could go out again?" He extracted a cell phone from his pocket. "What's your number? I'll call you."

With his hands on his phone and off my car door, I pulled it open. "I can't. I'm not who you think I am." I slid into the car and slammed the door closed, then reversed out of the parking space as fast as I could. In the rearview mirror, I saw him jam his hands into his pockets and watch me for a second. Then he crossed the parking lot to his own car.

Chapter 3

Saturday morning. Mom and I had both slept in. A week since the night of my date with Mason. I tried not to think about him when I sat alone in the evenings—after I put Mom to bed. He wasn't really my type. Not that I had a type. Because how could I have a type when I'd been on only a handful of dates in my entire life—most of them disasters? If I wanted a type, I had to go out and get it. Play the field. But I had no field. I didn't even have a tiny garden. Not even a planter box.

I was right to turn him down. Who knew what kind of guy he was on the inside.

My mom was my life. I didn't have time for anyone else, especially not someone who was in love with who I wasn't.

Love. Ha! We'd had one date. One. It was way too soon for that word—or any word. So why did I even think it? Why did I think about him at all? It wasn't me he was after anyway; it was my sister. She didn't deserve him.

"Don't worry, Mom. I'm not going anywhere." I brushed her bangs aside and kissed her forehead. "I'll always be here for you." I helped her into her daytime clothes—elastic waistband pants and a soft shirt.

I gripped her arm, helping her transfer from the bed to the wheelchair. "There you go. Now, what do you want for breakfast?"

She waved her hand, gesturing at something only she could see. "You'd better pick that up before your father gets home."

"Mom, Dad's gone. He's not ever coming home," I told her for the eight-millionth time.

"You know how he hates toys left out," she said.

I sighed. "I know. Don't worry. I'll pick it up."

She smiled with relief.

"How about some scrambled eggs and toast? You love that."

She didn't answer. Her eyes had gone glassy as she turned inside her mind.

I whisked two eggs into a bowl and added a splash of milk to make them fluffy—just like she'd taught me. The toast popped. I slathered it with real butter. She steadily lost weight, so anything to put some meat on her bones.

"Here comes breakfast." I carried her tray into the family room. She already had the TV up and running.

Someone knocked on the door. Other than rare and brief visits from Jennica, Millie was the only other person to cross that threshold in over three years.

I balanced the breakfast tray on one hand and opened the door.

He stood there with his hands still jammed in his pockets. Different pair of pockets though. And a different shirt. Without salad droppings.

"Mason?"

"Hey," he said.

I couldn't take my eyes off him. "What are you doing here?" My mom's eggs were getting cold. "Um, come in, I guess." I left the door open while I situated Mom and her food in the living room.

She unfolded the napkin and laid it across her lap. I wheeled her a few feet to the left into a warm patch of sunshine.

Mason had come in and quietly closed the door. When I turned my attention back to him, he was standing on the strip of linoleum entryway watching.

"Mom, this is Mason MacIntyre." I pointed at him. She was eating her eggs and didn't look up. "Remember him?"

She sipped her orange juice.

I used to apologize for her. I gave that up long ago. Why pretend things were not what they were? Mom seemed happy with her diminished life. No one hit her. No one yelled. No one smashed glasses on the kitchen walls. As far as I could tell, she was content.

I was sorry she couldn't remember people, but my regret was aimed back at me. I was sorry for myself, sorry that I'd lost my one real friend in this world.

Mason looked at me, then at my mom. He walked over and knelt in front of her chair. "Hi, Mrs. Ricks." He moved his head into her line of sight until her eyes focused on him. "It's nice to see you again."

She stared at him for a moment, then her attention drifted back to the television. She ate a bite of eggs and dabbed at her mouth with her napkin.

"Looks like a good breakfast," he said. "Scrambled eggs are my favorite. Especially with ketchup."

Her gaze locked on his. The glazing on her eyes shattered, replaced with a sharp look of fear. "We're out of ketchup," she whispered, struggling to get out of her chair. "I'm sorry. I'll go to the store. Five minutes."

I put a hand on her shoulder and turned her head so she was looking at me. "Mom, it's okay. This is Mason, remember? Dad's gone." Eight million and one.

Her struggles eased, and she glanced at him.

It took him about two seconds to respond. He smiled and shook his head. "I don't even want ketchup, I promise." He backed away—still on his knees—with his hands up, surrendering to my wheelchair-bound mother. "I'm totally fine without ketchup. In fact, I abhor condiments of all kinds. We're better off without them. All that sugar and . . . other ingredients. It's bad for your health."

I laughed out loud. Mason's retreat was priceless. Even Mom couldn't help smiling.

Then she blinked, and the moment was gone. Forgotten. Her mind strayed elsewhere, and she sipped her orange juice again.

"Come on," I said to Mason. "We can talk in the kitchen."

I checked one last time to make sure Mom was settled. She ate her breakfast while her soap opera played out on TV. She couldn't remember her husband was dead, but she knew which show she wanted to watch on which channel. I motioned Mason to follow me.

One of the few things I'd brought when I'd moved us out of our home in Cedar Springs was the old pine table that had belonged to my mother's mother. It had been scrubbed countless times but still bore the imprints of generations of fork wounds, homework, and tic-tac-toe.

I'd also brought the couch, our beds, and a few accessories. Nothing else would fit. Our house in the city had a kitchen, a living room, two bedrooms, and a bath. That was all we could afford. Luckily, that was all we needed.

"Have a seat," I said to Mason. "I'll make us some tea."

I took two mugs from the cupboard and strung a packet of herbal tea over the side of each. While the water heated, I sat at the table across from him. The smell of freshly shaved man spread through the kitchen, filling spaces I hadn't realized were empty. As far as I knew, the last male to sit at my grandmother's table was my father. Mason had taken his seat at the head, a spot easily identifiable by the gouges left from pounding silverware. Dinner had not always been the best time of day.

Mason—the epitome of tall, dark, and handsome—thankfully looked nothing like my dad. My father had the same reddish-auburn hair as Jennica and me. People always joked with us about the redheaded temper. We never laughed.

"I'm surprised to see you here this morning," I said. "How did you find me?"

He shrugged. "The Internet." He sounded a bit uncertain.

Plus, he was lying. If he'd looked me up on the Internet, he would have googled Jennica Ricks. That search would have taken him in a very different direction.

"The Internet?" I asked doubtfully.

"Actually, no." He blushed, an act that was not becoming of his masculine features. "The truth is, I followed you home Saturday night."

Okay. That was a little creepy. Also sort of cute. But mostly just weird.

"I didn't mean to," he explained. "At least not at first. It turns out we don't live that far apart. So by the time we'd made several of the same turns, I was curious."

I'd thought my not giving him my phone number at the restaurant had sent a clear message. When I'd pulled out of the parking lot, I'd assumed I'd never see him again. Now here he was, grinning at me sheepishly while his long limbs sprawled over the kitchen table.

I tried to muster some form of disappointment that my no-contact-information plan hadn't worked, but there was none to be found. And when the urge to lean in and smell him nearly overpowered me, I stood up to check the hot water.

Steam hissed from the kettle. I filled the two mugs. "Lemon tea," I said as I set the mug on the table in front of him. "I've got some honey here, but based on your disgust of all condiments, I doubt you'll want any."

He chuckled.

"Thanks for doing that, by the way. I never know when something will trigger a memory."

"It's no big deal." He squeezed some honey into his tea and stirred it. "It could happen to anyone."

I got the impression he was referring to the restaurant, when I spilled my salad on him. He probably wanted an explanation. A confession of life with an angry father. But if there was one thing I'd learned, it was to keep things to myself. Never expose a weakness. That was the exact spot they'd stab the dagger next.

My mother coughed softly in the next room. I should have gone to get her food tray and clean up breakfast, but I was enjoying sipping tea with Mason. This was the perfect opportunity for me to explain the identity mix-up. But how to begin? *Mason, by the way, remember that great time we had at the restaurant? It was all a lie. I'm not Jennica.* He'd never come sit in my kitchen again. Not that I wanted him to, I reminded myself. The big question was whether he would smash his mug on the floor once he learned he'd been deceived.

I had to say something. This had already gone on far too long. I opened my mouth to speak, but he beat me to it.

"How come you don't call me Mac?" he asked. "You used to always call me Mac; everyone did. Everyone still does except you."

My mother coughed again, louder this time, followed by the sound of dishes clattering to the floor.

I jumped up. "I better go check on her."

I rounded the corner of the wall that divided the kitchen from the living room to find my mother arching her back and gasping for breath.

"Mom?" I leapt over the fallen dishes and took her head between my hands. "Mom, what's wrong?" I tried to get her to focus on me. If ever she had a lucid moment, I needed it now.

She coughed again, a tight and pained cough that rattled in her chest. A dribble of blood seeped from her lips. She gasped, her hands pressed against her chest.

"Mom!"

"What's the matter?" Mason said from behind me.

"I don't know. She just started coughing, and now it's like she can't breathe." I showed him the napkin I'd used to wipe the blood off her mouth. In every movie I'd ever seen, life ended with blood leaking from the mouth.

He nudged me out of the way. With one arm, he lifted her, and with the other, he shoved the wheelchair out of the way, clearing a place for her on the floor.

"Has she been sick? Like pneumonia or anything?"

"No. She's been fine."

He dug into his pocket and handed me some keys. "Get my emergency kit from the backseat of my truck."

I ran out the door. He'd parked in the driveway, blocking the garage so I couldn't back out. Why I cared at that exact moment, I'd never know. I hit the unlock button twice and yanked open the rear driver's-side door.

Emergency kit? All I saw was an industrial-looking black case taking up most of the seat. I grabbed for it, but it weighed a ton. With both hands, I heaved it out of his truck and dragged it into the house.

Mason had Mom lying on her back on the floor. She was writhing and gasping. Her face had gone completely white.

Mason flipped open the case. The inside contained a miniature ER. He snapped on some latex gloves.

"Is she dying?" I asked, trying to keep my voice steady, though I failed. Even I could hear the hysterics crackling in my throat. "She's dying, isn't she? Oh my gosh. Mom!" I yelled.

Mason had taken a large silver cylinder out of his case. "She's going to be okay. You have to stay calm." He attached a small, clear mask to a long tube, then attached the tube to the cylinder. "Even though her faculties are diminished, if you panic, she'll know." He adjusted a dial on the top of the cylinder and put the mask over her nose and mouth. "Grace?" he said.

I didn't know how he knew her first name. I guessed from when he'd dated Jennica back in high school.

He kept his voice soft and reassuring, like he was soothing a frenzied animal. "I'm giving you oxygen. This will help you breathe."

The distant look in her eyes proved to me that she didn't understand a word he said. But either the gentleness of his voice or the oxygen seemed to relax her. She coughed again, and another clot of blood fell from her mouth.

"Mason, what's happening?"

"Here." He put my hand on the little oxygen mask. "Hold this. And keep her calm."

He pulled out his cell phone and punched three numbers. "Yes, I need an ambulance at 341 Wynder Street." He listened for a moment. "I have a female, late forties, having difficulty breathing. She's wheelchair bound, and I suspect APE." He went on to describe my mother's symptoms using a lot of medical terms. Then he listened again. "My name is Mason MacIntyre. I'm a first-year resident at Saint Mark's."

After a minute, he pushed the speaker button and laid his phone on the floor beside him. He took over the oxygen-mask job.

I held my mother's hands, hoping to keep her nerves steady. "She's burning up."

She started writhing again, her eyes wide and her chest heaving for breath. Then she went completely still. "Mom!" I screamed, shaking her body. "Mason, do something."

He looped the elastic around her head to hold the oxygen mask in place. With two fingers on her neck, he checked her pulse. After a small adjustment to the oxygen flow, he leaned in close and listened.

"She's just unconscious. That's her body's way of saying, 'Hey, I'm not getting all the oxygen I need, so I'll turn off anything that's not necessary.'" He checked her heart rate again. "Her pulse is getting stronger, and she's breathing better. The ambulance will be here soon; she'll be okay."

"What's wrong with her? What's AEP or whatever?"

"APE. Acute pulmonary embolism. It's when blood pools in the veins of the legs and forms a sort of clot. Sometimes those clots dislodge and travel to other vital organs and cause problems. In your mother's case, her lungs. It's blocking respiration. She can't get enough oxygen, and carbon dioxide is building in her blood stream."

"Will she die?"

"No." He looked at me. Right into my eyes. The moment he came into the living room and found my mom gasping for air, he'd gone into some kind of medical mode—all business and efficiency—but now, as he watched me, his face softened. "People die from this, yes. But not your mom. Not today." He peeled the latex gloves off his hands and wadded them up.

A siren sounded in the neighborhood and grew louder.

He picked up his phone and told the operator he was hanging up now because the ambulance was here. Then he turned to me. "She's stable. The ambulance will be here any moment. They'll give her an anticoagulant to prevent the clot from building. She'll be okay. I promise." He smiled at me very convincingly.

Chapter 4

Mom lay sleeping in her bed at Riverside General Hospital. Her soft, rhythmic breathing was the most comforting sound in the world. She'd spent most of the day in tests and scans, and by the time they'd wheeled her in here, she was exhausted.

Her face had some color again, thanks to the oxygen tubes and IVs coiled around her, and every few minutes the mechanical hum of leg compressors filled the room.

The doctor had told me this was all my fault.

Well, he hadn't exactly said that. But, apparently, I should have been helping her exercise more. I should have been making her stand up more often. I should have been putting support socks on her legs so blood clots wouldn't form. The reduced-rate clinic we'd been going to had failed to mention any of that.

Some caretaker I was. I'd practically killed my own mother.

During her scan, I'd stepped outside and called Jennica, filling her in on what had happened and Mom's condition. She confirmed what the doctor had said, blaming me for being negligent about our mom's needs. I told her if I was so bad, maybe she should come home and take over. "Maybe I will," she'd said.

There was a soft knock on the door, and Mason came in. "Hey, there. How are you holding up?"

I shrugged. "Fine."

I could have supplied quite an addendum to my answer of how I was holding up, but any expatiating would have resulted in a complete emotional breakdown. I'd almost lost my mother. I turned and looked out the window so he wouldn't see my face contorting into the I'm-not-going-to-cry expression.

The night was settling in, transforming the streets below into a Milky Way of headlights and street lamps. "They said you saved her life. Thanks. You really are a hero."

"Just lucky, I suppose."

I could hear him fiddling around with her monitor and checking the compression pump.

"Lucky I happened to be there. And lucky I'm pigheaded enough to carry that emergency kit with me. It cost me an arm and a leg, and everyone said it was overkill, but it sure came in handy today."

I nodded. Having Mason at my house the moment we'd needed him went beyond luck. It seemed more like divine intervention.

"What if it happens again?" I asked. "Or something else? Doing copyedits on my computer with soap operas blaring in the background hasn't exactly prepared me for serious life-and-death situations." I leaned my head against the cool glass of the window. "I should've taken better care of her. Then none of this would have happened."

He came around the bed and stood beside me. "Listen, I only had to be in your house for two minutes to see how good of a caretaker you are. You're amazing. Most people would have checked their parent into a nursing home a long time ago."

I looked up at him. "At least she would have been safe there."

"Maybe. But probably not happy. All things considered, she seems pleased with her life. I saw how she smiles at you. How she calms when you hold her hand. She may not be able to express it, but she loves you. That much is clear."

The compression pump released its air with a soft whoosh, and the room went quiet. I turned back to the window.

I'd spent hours and hours wondering what went through her mind. Did she even know I was there, dressing her, cooking for her, helping her to the bathroom?

Mason thought she knew. He said she loved me. I wanted that to be true. Caring for her was hard but gratifying. I didn't mind giving back some of what she'd given me—a place of safety. It was a full-time, around-the-clock, no-vacation-days-or-holidays endeavor. Today, it left me weary to the bone.

He reached out and stilled my twisting hands. I'd nearly rubbed my thumb raw during the course of the day. "You don't have to do everything alone, you know. You can let your friends help."

With the softest touch on my shoulder, he pulled me close. I didn't resist. I fell into his embrace like it was some kind of fulcrum—a single, stable point that balanced out all the craziness . . . and all the loneliness.

I hadn't realized how stretched thin I'd become. The strength of Mason's embrace unarmed me. All the fear and stress of the day broke free, gushing out in wet sobs quickly soaked up by his shirt.

He didn't seem to mind. He held me quietly, one hand on my back and the other smoothing my hair.

He had to be as exhausted as I was; he'd been with us at the hospital most of the day, but it didn't show.

"Thank you so much for all your help today," I said once I got my voice back. "I don't know what I would have done if I'd had to deal with this by myself."

"No problem." He lowered his gaze to my face. "I'm just grateful your mom waited until my day off."

He was so close. I couldn't look away. Something changed in his eyes as he watched me; they filled with warmth and longing. Or was that the reflection of my eyes in his? I couldn't tell.

How did he still smell so good after this long and difficult day? I was sure I smelled like desperation. His whiskers were coming in dark and bristly along his jawline. I reached up and ran the back of my fingers along them, making a faint sandpapery sound.

"Jennica," he whispered.

Bam. The spell was broken. With everything that had happened, I'd forgotten that he still thought I was my sister.

I stepped away. "Oh my goodness, look at the time." I spun around until I found the clock on the wall and pointed. "I can't believe this thing with my mom took up your whole day."

He seemed taken aback for a moment, then his hands went to their usual resting place—stuffed into his pants pockets. He looked at the clock as if it were the most fascinating thing he'd ever seen. Then he pulled out one of his hands and rubbed his jaw in the same place I'd been stroking only seconds ago.

"Sorry," he said. "I shouldn't have . . . I overstepped. I didn't mean . . ."

"No. It's just that . . . Well." I twisted and pulled at my thumb. Everything was awkward now. It filled my mother's hospital room like rolling thunder until I worried it would wake her. I might as well round out the awkwardness with a long-overdue confession. "I'm not the girl you dated in high school." There. I said it.

He nodded. "I know. You've changed so much. I can't believe it. We've got a lot of catching up to do." He spoke quickly, as if he could silence the awkwardness with words. "Let's not get into all that right now. You look ready to drop." He glanced down at my sleeping mother. "Go home and get some rest. I'll stay with your mom."

"What? No." How did we end up here, talking about my mom? I couldn't just leave. I needed to clarify who I was. At the same time, I was so tired I could barely stand. "No. I should stay. In case she wakes up."

Mason put his hand on the small of my back and steered me toward the door. "I insist. I promise I'll call you if she wakes up or if anything changes."

"But—"

"I insist," he said again. He gave me the briefest glimpse of that earnest look again. "You don't have to do everything alone. I want to help."

All I needed was a few hours of uninterrupted sleep. I'd spent enough time with my mom after the accident to know that such a thing did not exist in a hospital.

Would it really make that big of a difference if I saved my confession a tiny bit longer? It might go better if we had some rest and some space between us.

"Okay. Just a few hours." I looked around for my purse and keys. That was when I realized I didn't have them. I'd ridden here in the ambulance. I had no way home.

Mason pulled his keys out of his pocket and handed them to me. "Take my truck."

"Then how will you get home?"

"You drive it here when you come back."

"Then how will I get home?"

He rolled his eyes. "You're so tired your mind is cracking. Just go."

I didn't know what else to do, so I shook his hand. "Thanks. And especially thanks for this morning."

* * *

I emerged from a blurry sleep, confused about why I was on the couch in the living room. Then I remembered I'd lain there instead of on my bed so I wouldn't sleep too long. I checked the time. Eight hours! Oh my gosh. I couldn't believe I'd left Mason all night with my mother. He had to be going out of his mind.

Or he'd left.

What guy would sit that long at the hospital with somebody else's parent?

I ran into the bathroom and brushed my teeth while simultaneously pulling my unwilling hair into a ponytail. I spilled toothpaste on my shirt and had to make a quick wardrobe change.

Mason's truck waited for me in the driveway. I drove as fast as I could back to the hospital. It was Sunday. Did Mason have to work today? If so, he might have had to leave.

The elevator dinged open, and I hurried down the hall. The light was off, so I entered quietly in case she was resting.

A food tray with a half-eaten breakfast had been pushed off to the side, and Mom lay sleeping with the TV remote clutched in her hand. Mason also slept, his large frame curled up on the vinyl reclining chair. He had a pillow stuffed under his head, and his blanket had slipped off everything but his feet. The quiet whir of Mom's leg compressors blended nicely with his soft snores.

"Mason?" I touched him on the shoulder. "I'm sorry I'm late."

He snorted in his sleep.

"Mason."

"Huh?" He sat up, slowly unfolding his body from the cramped position.

"I'm really sorry I overslept."

"Oh." He checked his watch. "Oh," he said again. Then he smiled at me. A real smile, with crinkly eyes and everything. He looked at me for a long time, grinning like he'd just won the lottery. No man had ever looked at me like that before. I was glad it wasn't my heart hooked up to the monitors.

Last night's five o'clock shadow had grown into the beginnings of a hearty beard. His dark hair stuck straight up on the side of his head that had lain on the pillow. He'd never looked more attractive to me than he did at that moment. I must have been staring, because his smile broadened. I couldn't take my eyes off the way his lips looked so soft and smooth surrounded by the scruff of whiskers.

"No problem," he finally said. "We've been doing just fine here, haven't we, Grace?" There was no response from the bed. "I guess she fell back asleep."

I set my purse down on the bedside stand and handed him his keys. "When did she wake up? Why didn't you call me?"

Mason finger-combed his hair and tugged his clothes back into order. "She woke up a few hours ago. I called, but you didn't answer."

I checked the history on my phone. I had missed a call from an unidentified number. "Sorry," I said. "I must have slept through it."

"That's what I figured. And since she was fine, I didn't worry about it. You needed to rest."

His info on my phone made me realize that in my stupor last night, I'd neglected to give him my contact information. "How did you find my number?" I asked.

He pointed to the white board on the wall the nurse had filled out. It stated the name of the primary care physician, the nurse on duty, and the emergency contact information.

There, in blue dry-erase marker were the words *Jane (daughter)* and my phone number.

"Except they put Jane instead of Jen." He laughed at the incompetency of it all.

"Uh, yeah." I hung my head. He thought he was helping out an old friend, but all this time, he'd been helping me, a stranger. I'd lose him if I told the truth, which wasn't saying much because he wasn't mine to lose.

I sat across from him on the edge of Mom's bed and maneuvered the tray table until it formed a barrier between us. My confession would make him mad; I just didn't know how mad. I wanted to be prepared. "About that."

He nodded, only half paying attention as he loosened the laces to put on his shoes.

"My name is Jane."

"What?" he said, although I could tell his mind was preoccupied with other thoughts.

"Jennica is my sister."

"What?" This time his head snapped up. "What sister?"

Exactly. Four months, I think they dated, and she never mentioned me once. "Jennica is my twin sister."

I sounded like an idiot—because I was an idiot. I should have told him from the very beginning instead of waiting until all I wanted was to experience the contrast of smooth lips and stubbly whiskers. But then he wouldn't have taken me to dinner, and he wouldn't have followed me home, and he wouldn't have been there when Mom had had her attack. So in reality, hiding under my sister's assumed identity had saved my mother's life.

He leaned back in his chair like he'd had the wind knocked out of him. "Identical twins?"

I nodded.

"Why didn't you tell me?" His smile was gone, and he narrowed his lips until they disappeared into a ring of dark bristles.

"I don't know. I meant to. I tried a few times, but obviously not hard enough . . . I'm just stupid, I guess." There was no logical explanation. Only stupidity. And stupidity is hard to explain away. It's something that starts as a logical thought but quickly grows out of control, taking over everything like a self-destroying, flesh-eating disease. "I had a silly crush on you all through high school, so at the grocery store when you asked me out—or when you asked Jennica out or whatever—I couldn't resist." That was the only reasoning I had.

He stared at me, examining every inch of my face. "You look exactly like her."

"Yes. That's where the identical part comes in."

He didn't smile. "You could have said something at dinner."

"I thought about it. But I was having a good time, and I wanted it to last." One lame excuse after another. "I knew you'd get angry and leave."

He leaned down and tied his shoes. "That's what you knew? That I'd get angry and storm out of the restaurant or something?"

"Or something."

The nurse knocked on the door and came in. I jumped up. Mason did the same. We stood there like uncomfortable statues while the nurse took my mom's vitals and told me everything looked good. She informed us that the doctor would be in soon to discuss long-term treatment and such. With one last check of the monitor, she left.

Mom stirred. She opened her eyes and looked straight through me. Then she bolted up and swiped at the tubes, trying to pull her IV out and strip the oxygen from her nose.

Mason leapt to the bedside. I held down her hands while he checked her IV.

"Mom."

She looked up at me.

"You have to leave those in, okay? They're helping you get better."

Mason slipped her oxygen back on, looping the tubing around her ears.

"Jane?" she asked.

"Yes." I couldn't believe she'd gotten it right. "You're in the hospital because you had a blood clot in your lungs. Do you remember that?"

She nodded even as that far-off look crept into her eyes.

"Mom." I forced myself into her field of vision. "Stay with me. How are you feeling?"

"I'm fine. But you should check on your father. He won't be happy if no one's home to fix his lunch."

Just when I thought I might have her for a few moments, she slipped away. I didn't even bother to explain again that Dad was gone. "Okay, Mom. I'll fix him lunch."

Mason flicked her IV line a few times and watched it drip, drip, drip. "No harm done."

"Did she do that when she woke up this morning?"

"Nope. She was a perfect lady. We had a lovely talk about the church picnic and your upcoming trip to Mount Rushmore. Then we shared a delicious breakfast of powdered eggs, frozen sausage, dry toast, warm orange juice, and canned fruit." He laughed just like he'd done before I'd told him the truth. "Then she turned on the TV and fell asleep."

"That sounds like Mom. No matter what's going on around her, she has to have her shows. I suppose they were her escape when Dad was alive. And now they're her link to the real world—as strange as that sounds."

Mason gave my mom's hand a little squeeze, then leveled his eyes on me. "So."

The reprieve had ended. We were back to the sticky conversation about lies and truth. He'd managed his anger well so far, kept it tucked away and the wolf chained up. I wanted to keep it that way.

"So," I said. "I guess that's it. Thanks again for saving my mom. And for staying with her all night. I would have been lost without you." And I would be again after he walked through that door. "And I'm sorry. For not being up-front about the whole Jennica thing."

"Yeah." He looked around the room, searching for something, even though the place was empty—except for my mother and the medical equipment. "The thing is . . ." His hands turned into fists, which he thrust into his pockets.

A reminder to me that I should move my own hands behind my back. He didn't need to see me twisting them as we said good-bye. We stood there for a while, avoiding eye contact. Not speaking.

He sighed, then pulled out his wallet. "Here's my card if you ever need anything. Like help with your mom and whatnot. Or someone to talk to."

The business card he handed me had the St. Mark's logo in the top right corner and "Dr. Mason MacIntyre, Emergency Medicine" in blue across the middle.

When I looked up, he was gone. I ran around Mom's bed and pulled the door open. I almost called out, but in the end, I didn't know what to say.

Life was infinitely better when he was around. He was like a patch of blue sky through the thick fog that closed in on me day by day. But I wasn't the sister he wanted. So I watched him walk away.

Chapter 5

Mom had to stay in the hospital for a week. They tapered off the heparin she'd been getting through the IV, then started her on an oral anticoagulant. They tested her blood endlessly, trying to get the dose right. I was going to have to mortgage the house to pay the hospital bills.

I'd spent most of my days here with her. I'd tried to stay the nights too, but I just couldn't. It exhausted me. I slept at home with strict instructions to be informed immediately of any problems.

Mom didn't seem to mind the hospital stay. She had a TV and around-the-clock care. What else did she need?

The week had rolled around to Saturday again. I hadn't seen Mason at all. I suspected that at least one evening—maybe more—he'd come to the hospital to see my mother, but I'd already gone home for the night. The nurse mentioned something about Dr. MacIntyre checking in. I didn't ask for more details.

Mom's discharge was today. I packed up my belongings that had accumulated during her stay. At least I'd gotten a lot of work done while sitting with her.

"Dr. Mac?" Mom said, glancing around the room.

"He's not here," I answered before I fully realized who Mom was asking for. I didn't know she'd ever comprehended his existence. "He had to leave."

"That's too bad. He's very good looking."

"Yes. Yes, he is."

"Do you think he'll come say good-bye before we go?"

Wow. She even remembered about leaving. She was full of surprises this morning. "I doubt it. He works at a different hospital." It had been a long time since I'd had a conversation with my mother where we were both in the present.

"He tickled me."

Maybe she wasn't as fully present as I'd thought. "He tickled you?"

"He said laughter was the best medicine, then he tickled my feet."

I tried to picture Mason's fingers skimming across my mother's feet. "Did you laugh?" I asked.

"Yes. You know how ticklish my feet are."

I did. She used to always wear shoes just so she wouldn't get tickled.

"Your father used to tickle me all the time. He said my laugh was his favorite sound. That was before we married, of course. When we were still dating."

I'd never seen my father do anything playful with my mother. Maybe he had, and those memories had just been buried under all the other stuff.

"Do you regret marrying him, Mom?" If she could rewind time, would she steer clear of the Big Bad Wolf? He'd made her life a living hell, but I'd never once heard her complain.

She lifted my hand and held it close to her heart. "You are the joy of my life. I wouldn't trade that for anything. I love you so much."

I leaned in and hugged her as tightly as I dared. "I love you too," I whispered.

Her hold on me relaxed. "And when you're done with your homework, you can go back outside and play."

That was it. That one moment was all I got. Now she was gone, lost in her mind again.

"Let's get you dressed." I helped her into her clothes and combed her hair—the only thing about her that spoke her true age. It was a beautiful dark brown, healthy and luminous, free of grays.

The nurse came in with the last bit of instructions and a stack of papers for me to sign. She helped me shift Mom into a wheelchair, and then she pushed her slowly toward the elevator while I ran ahead to pull my car around to the front of the hospital.

As I neared home, a familiar vehicle sat parked in the driveway—Mason's truck. He must have found out we were coming home today. I would be glad for his help getting Mom into the house.

I parked on the curb. Before leaving the car, I lowered the visor and checked the mirror. I hadn't put makeup on, and my hair was pulled up in a messy bun. Oh well. Nothing I could do about it now.

"Wait here, Mom. I'm going to get your chair. I'll be right back."

I expected to see Mason sitting behind the wheel of his truck, waiting for me to get home with Mother. It was empty. I'd locked the house when I'd left that morning, so perhaps he'd gone for a walk or into the backyard. Or had I forgotten to lock the house? Would he just walk in?

I tried the doorknob, and it turned. I pushed the door open and stepped quietly inside.

There, right on the couch where I watched TV with my mother, sat Mason.

He didn't see me. He was already occupied. His dark hair had fallen forward, twining with another head of hair—not quite red but not auburn either.

Jennica.

Mason was kissing Jennica. She must have pulled her car into the garage. That's why I hadn't seen it.

Mason wasn't here for me. He was here for her.

If I hadn't had my invalid mother waiting in the car, I would have slipped away unseen. But I had to move her inside, and I couldn't do that with Mason and Jennica having a high school reunion on the couch.

"Mason?" I said.

His head whipped around. He flew off the couch. "What the—?" He looked back and forth between the two of us, my twin sister and me. "Jennica?" he said to me.

Jennica gracefully lifted herself. She grinned. "Hi, Jane. Long time no see." No wonder they got along so well together.

"Jane?" Mason asked. "But I thought—"

"You thought what?" I said. "That we'd be at the hospital a little longer?" He had shaved that morning, leaving his face much smoother than the last time I'd seen it. The smell of his aftershave wafted about. I wanted to bottle it up, but then I realized it was already bottled before he'd put it on.

"No." He studied Jennica, then me. "Jane?" he asked again.

"Yes, I'm Jane; she's Jennica. The one you were kissing." I shouldn't have been upset. I had no claim to him, and it had been Jennica he'd been excited to go out with in the first place. I'd lied to him, so how could I possibly expect anything other than what I deserved?

Somehow, in our short time together, Mason had me believing he was different. But no, he'd turned out just like everyone else. Charming and sweet at first, then hello, Mr. Wolf. Well, he and Jennica deserved each other.

"Jane, I'm sorry." He took two steps toward me but stopped when I backed away. "I made a mistake. I thought—"

"Mason. You don't have to explain anything. You wanted to go out with Jennica; now's your chance." I gave him a wide berth as I made my way to Mom's bedroom. Jennica watched like she was enjoying a Tony award–winning production. I wheeled Mom's chair out and headed for the front door. "My mom's waiting in the car."

He tried to take over pushing the chair. "Here, let me help."

"No!" I shouted, then lowered my voice. "No, thanks. I can manage. You should probably go. Mom's really tired."

He let go of the chair.

Jennica gave Mason a wry smile. "See ya, Mac." She opened the door for me, and I pushed the wheelchair out and down the ramp. I heard the front door slam. Then Mason's truck door slammed. He revved his engine and backed out of the driveway.

Jennica helped me transfer Mom into her wheelchair, then she pushed her into the house while I unloaded the rest of the stuff. She took Mom into her bedroom, ready to help her into bed.

"I don't think she'll want to be in bed," I said.

Jennica snorted. "How can you tell what she wants and doesn't want. She's comatose."

"She's not comatose." I glared at Jennica before leaning down and asking Mom, "Are you tired? Do you want to lie down, or do you want to come sit with us?"

"My shows are on," Mom said. "I'll just watch until your father gets home."

"See?" Jennica said. "Wacko."

Jerk. I didn't say it, but I thought it hard enough that I'm sure it showed on my face. I put Mom in front of the TV and gave her the remote control. "You know, Jen, maybe if you actually spent some time with her, you'd see she still has good moments." Like this morning in the hospital.

"No, thanks. Like I have time to waste lolling around here," Jennica said. "But let's not talk about Mom. I want to hear all about you and Mason MacIntyre."

Of course she did. She never missed a chance to gloat. "There's nothing to tell."

Jennica followed me into the kitchen. I yanked open the fridge and fished out what I needed to make a sandwich for Mom. Jennica snatched the tomato out of my hand and started slicing.

Her presence always put me in a conundrum. When she wasn't around, and I had to care for Mom alone, I missed her. I wished she would come home and help. When she was here, I remembered why we were better off without her. The reason Jennica got along with people like Dad and Mason was that she understood the wolf mentality. She had it too.

She smirked at me. "Then why did he call me Jane? And why did he ask for a chance to start over?"

"He said that?" Oops. I hadn't meant to show so much interest. *Don't expose any weakness*, I reminded myself. *That's where she'll stab the dagger next.*

"Ha!" she said with triumph. "I knew there was something." She sawed back and forth with a serrated knife.

"Well, Jen, you are mistaken." I tried to keep my voice cool.

I hadn't been to the store in a week, and the bread was moldy. Mom would have to have her sandwich on a tortilla, wrap style.

Jennica narrowed her eyes at me. Calculating. Her internal gauge swung from crafty all the way up to devious. I could see it clearly in her face. "He did seem happy to see me," she said. "We had such good times back in the day."

I spread some mayonnaise on the tortilla and added just a skim of mustard. Jennica was working hard to get under my skin. The more I didn't react, the sooner this would be over. Next time Mom almost died, I would not be calling her. She made everything worse. I placed the turkey, tomato, and lettuce on the tortilla and rolled it up.

Jennica would poke and prod until I ended up either in tears or screaming at her. That was how she operated. She didn't have much self-control of her own, so when people resisted her torture, I think she took it as a personal challenge to reduce them to her level.

"Mac said at first he thought you were me." She made it sound like an insult. "He couldn't believe he'd made that mistake because we are nothing alike." She paused, watching my face.

Mason must have talked for her to know that detail. I kept my eyes on the lunch, opening the fridge for a protein shake to complete the meal.

"He said he was surprised at how naive and immature you are. I think that's why he ended up back with me."

She was going for tears. I already felt my eyes stinging. Of course he would think that. I hadn't even had the gumption to tell him my own name. But I wouldn't let Jennica win this round, not this time.

"We're going out again," she told me. "Before I have to leave. I think he just might be the one."

"Great," I snapped, lifting the food tray. "I hope everything works out for you two." I pushed past her into the living room.

"Here's your lunch, Mom." I attached the tray to her chair. She still looked a little pale from the ride home, and when I squeezed her hand, it was ice cold. I pushed her into the patch of sunshine, though the sun was moving fast and it wouldn't last long. I draped a blanket around her as well. "It's good to be home, right?"

She smiled up at me, her eyes lost and distant.

Jennica cleared her throat. "Mac also said—"

"You know what? It's been a long week. Make yourself useful for a change and sit here with Mom. I need a nap." I didn't wait for an answer. I walked away, closed and locked my bedroom door, and collapsed onto my bed.

I didn't nap. My blood seethed. I had to get my mind on something else. I pulled one of my favorite books from the shelf: *The Tenant of Wildfell Hall.* I flipped straight to the best part, where Helen takes her young son and steals away into the Yorkshire countryside, escaping the clutches of her abusive husband.

A scandalous novel in its time. Even though Helen's self-righteousness bordered on obscene, I couldn't help cheering for her. She had extraordinary courage—something I greatly lacked. Was she born with it? Or did she acquire it through practice, like playing the piano? Maybe it had been forced on her by years of living with such a vile man. When she could bear his depravations no longer, perhaps she had reached down deep inside and found something that hadn't been there before: the courage to break away.

Just as the honorable Mr. Markham was about to declare his love to Helen, shouts came from the living room. I closed the book and listened.

"No!" Mom yelled, who as far as I knew hadn't raised her voice in her entire life, especially not since the accident. I jumped off the bed and opened my door to hear better.

"I'm not watching any more of your idiotic shows," Jennica said. "American Idol is on."

I walked down the hall to find Jennica wrestling with my mother to get the remote. Mom clutched it with both hands tightly to her chest.

Jennica stood up, fury burning in her face. "Give me the remote."

Mom shook her head.

Yellow fire flared in Jennica's eyes. She hadn't seen me enter the room with all her attention centered on Mom. "Give it to me, or you'll be sorry."

I lunged forward and blocked Jennica's hand just in time to prevent her slap from landing on Mom's face.

She jerked her arm out of my grip. She looked just like Dad as she smiled lovingly at me. "Jane, how was your nap?"

"Get out," I said.

"What?"

"Get out. Get your things and leave."

Her adoring facade melted away. "You have no right to tell me to leave."

I took a step back, afraid of what I saw in her eyes. People always said we looked exactly alike, but I hoped I never looked like that. "This is my house, and I want you out."

She stared at me. Tears welled up and trickled down her face. She wiped them away, but more quickly followed. "I'm so sorry, Jane. I didn't mean to hurt her. I don't know what came over me. I'm just so tired from driving all night to get here." She slumped onto the couch. At least her acting skills weren't going to waste. "Please don't put me out on the street. I have nowhere else to go. Please. I love Mom. It won't ever happen again. I promise."

Jennica looked at me pleadingly. "I want to help you take care of her. I'm just trying to think of what's best for her. She almost died, Jane. Think of how much safer she'll be if we do it together."

I bent down to check on Mom. Other than a few scratches where Jennica had clawed for the remote, she seemed okay. She had gone back to her shows. For once, I hoped her mind was very far away, that she understood nothing of what had just happened.

The idea of not having to do this alone sounded like heaven to me. But if Jennica thought I'd learned nothing from watching my dad for more than twenty-one years, she was mistaken. All our lives, Jennica had had a temper. Until now, I'd never seen it like this. She'd stepped into my father's shoes effortlessly. I wouldn't live like that ever again.

"You can't stay here," I said. "Get your stuff and go."

"Now?" she asked. She didn't fool me with her look of contrition.

"Now." I put my hands on the back of Mom's wheelchair. "I'm taking Mom to bed. When I come out, I want you gone."

"Where am I supposed to go?"

"Wherever you want." I pushed Mom down the hall, away from the living room.

Jennica called after me. "Fine. Mac said he had a spare room. He'd love to help me out. Maybe I'll go stay with him."

I shut my mother's door. Ten minutes later, I heard the garage open and close. Jennica was gone.

Chapter 6

Other than Mom's new medicines and support socks, the next day we were back to life as usual. I gave her a bath and breakfast, explained again that Dad was gone, and set her in front of the TV.

I plopped onto the couch, careful to avoid the site of the Mason-Jennica fiasco, and went to work on my computer. Never before had copyediting brought me so much comfort. Last week, with Mom's illness, Mason's betrayal, and Jennica's wolfish behavior, my world had fallen out of alignment. Life didn't care. It pressed on unabated. Today, everything seemed back to normal.

My phone rang. I checked the caller ID. Mason. My stupid heart betrayed me, thumping in my chest and sending my brain unwanted visions of his blue eyes and scruffy face. Was Jennica staying with him? How many lies would she have told him by now?

Stop it! I wasn't going there again. I pushed ignore.

What else was there for us to say? No matter how many excuses or apologies Mason and I threw at each other, it added up to the same thing. We'd both done wrong by each other.

A few days later, he called again. I didn't answer. The sooner I got over him, the better. I already had plans for Friday night. Dinner and a movie. All by myself.

"Stop moping," Mom said. She'd been watching TV—or so I'd thought—when all of a sudden she looked right at me and said it again. "Stop moping."

"What?" Did she mean me or the teary-eyed nurse on her show?

"It's not attractive. If you miss the doctor that much, go after him."

"Are you talking to me? Or Nurse Abigail?" I still wasn't sure.

"I'm talking to you."

"But I . . . He doesn't like me. He likes Jennica. He's always been interested in Jennica. Obviously." He'd made that very clear.

"There's always something," Mom said, turning back to the TV. "He's interested in someone else. No one would choose me. I'm not his type. Excuses. Do you think everything you want will just land in your lap? It doesn't work that way, honey."

"Are you suggesting I call him?" That surprised me coming from her. Well, this whole conversation surprised me, but aside from that . . . After her experience with settling for the wrong guy, I never thought she'd be encouraging me to ignore the warning signs.

"It doesn't matter that he already adopted your sister's baby."

"What?" Had she been talking to the TV this whole time? "Come on, Mother." I turned her program off. "I think you've had enough Lifetime Television for one day."

* * *

I opened my eyes. Something had roused me from sleep. I checked my clock. Almost three in the morning.

"Jane," came a weak voice from my mother's room.

I threw the covers off and hurried in. She never called me during the night. In fact, the one thing I could always count on from her was a long and peaceful night's rest.

She gripped her chest. Another embolism? I thought the anticoagulants were supposed to prevent that. Her breathing sounded fine, and her color was good—nothing like last time. "What's wrong?"

"It hurts," she whispered.

"What hurts? Where?"

Her hands fluttered above her body for a moment, then she pointed to her hip.

"Your hip?"

She pointed lower.

"Your leg?"

She nodded.

Maybe a new clot was forming. "I'm calling 911."

"No!" she said with about as much insistence as I'd heard from her in a long time, the remote control incident aside. "Call the doctor. He'll know what to do."

I wasn't exactly sure who she meant, but I suspected. "What doctor?"

"Doctor Mac. He'll know what to do."

"I'm not calling Mason. That's final."

She grabbed my arm. "Call him." She groaned.

Ever since her embolism, she'd been different—a little less wandery and a little more here and now. She so rarely asked for anything, how could I ignore her?

I toggled through my contacts until I found Mason's number. I couldn't believe I was doing this, at three in the morning no less.

"Hello?" a groggy voice said.

"Mason? It's Jane."

Silence for a moment, then, "Jane. Hey. Is everything okay?"

"Um, no. Not really. My mom's having some weird pains. I'm so sorry to call at this hour, but she insisted."

"She asked for me?" He sounded surprised. I didn't blame him. This whole thing was so far out of my mother's usual MO that I wondered if she needed her meds adjusted.

"I'm sorry. I should have said no. This was a stupid idea. Just forget about it." My finger hovered over the end-call button until I heard Mason again.

"Jane? Hold your horses." He asked me some specific questions about her breathing and color, then said, "I'll be there. Just give me a second."

Mason in my house. Was I ready for this?

"Jane? Are you there?" he asked.

"I'm here."

"Okay, I'm coming. See you soon." Then he hung up.

I went back into Mom's room. She seemed about the same—just sort of lying there, letting out a soft, occasional moan. After a while, she asked for some water.

I hurried to the kitchen, got a glass, and filled it with cool water from the fridge. As I started back to her room, the doorbell rang.

Mason.

He jiggled the handle, but it was dead-bolted. I fumbled with it, trying not to spill the water. It unlocked, and I opened the door.

He hadn't combed his hair. His baggy sweatpants bunched around his ankles, and his T-shirt had faded to something close to gray. Still, he was the best-looking guy I'd ever seen. Even for three in the morning.

"Jane." He nodded at me.

"Come in."

He had his big black emergency kit, and he carried it straight to my mother's room. I stood on one side of her bed while Mason worked on the other.

He checked her breathing, listened to her heart. "Grace?"

She looked at him.

"What's wrong? Where does it hurt?"

"Something's wrong with my leg," she said. "It feels like a horse."

Mason and I glanced at each other. "She said from the beginning that she had a pain in her leg," I told him. "I thought maybe she was getting another clot."

"I'd be surprised because of her medications, but it's possible." He pulled the sheets down and lifted the leg my mom had pointed to. "Did she have leg pain like this before the embolism?"

"No, not that she mentioned. But she doesn't always tell me everything."

He examined her leg carefully. "Color looks good, doesn't feel warm, no swelling in her ankle. Does this hurt?" he asked her.

She shook her head.

Thank goodness she was still with it. I'd worried that by the time Mason got here, Mom's mind would have wandered off and she wouldn't be able to answer his questions.

He flexed her foot, stretching and massaging Mom's calf muscle. She sighed and closed her eyes. Within half a minute, she was sound asleep.

"What happened? Is she okay?"

Mason smiled up at me, almost laughing. "She was right."

"Right about what?"

"Her leg did feel like a horse. A charley horse." He pulled her blankets up and tucked her in. "A leg cramp in her calf. When I stretched the muscle, it went away."

He packed up his emergency kit and snapped it shut. "If you have a heating pad, you might put that on it to keep the muscle relaxed. And given her history, her doctor may still want to run some tests to completely rule out thrombosis, but she didn't have any of the usual signs, other than the muscle cramp."

That was it. I'd called Mason over in the middle of the night for a charley horse. Good thing I hadn't called the ambulance. We left Mom sleeping and shuffled down the hall into the living room, toward the door.

"I'm sorry I ruined your night for that."

He shook his head. "You didn't ruin my night. You did the right thing. I'm glad you called."

"Well, now I know what to do so next time I won't have to." I tried to put my hands behind my back, but they insisted on remaining in front, twisting and pulling.

"Next time, you call me. Okay?" He took one of my hands in his, putting an end to their worrying.

I pulled away. All I could think about was Jennica and him. Had she left town? Or was she camped out on Mason's couch? "How's Jen?"

He shrugged. "I don't know. Haven't heard from her since we . . . well, you know. The day your mom came home."

"You seemed really happy to see her." Why couldn't he just admit that she was the one who interested him?

He set his hefty case on the ground. "She lied to me. You know that, right? She pretended to be you."

Just like I'd done when I'd pretended to be her. At what point had I become desperate enough to stoop to her level? Dad's level. No wonder she was the only family member to escape his wrath. My father recognized one of his own.

Anyway, Mason had said Jennica and I were very different. If that was true, how could I believe he kissed her without knowing who she was? It didn't seem to me she'd had to work very hard to lure him in.

"You should go," I said. "I'll tell my mom you said good-bye."

He seemed surprised by that. And a little bugged.

I pressed on. "Clean breaks are always best. As a doctor, you should already know that."

Something changed in his face. He raised his hands into the air, fists tight. "For the love of Pete! Why are you so frustrating?"

Oops. I'd woken the wolf.

I turned away, shielding my face, bracing for what was to come. "I'm sorry. I didn't mean it."

The room stalled as though someone had pushed the pause button. Mason's measured breathing was all I could hear.

"Jane?" he whispered. He walked around until he faced me. Before I had time to react, he slipped his arms around me, pulling me close. "I don't know what happened to you or who made you this way, but I promise you one thing: I will never hurt you."

I nodded as best I could pressed up against him. I wanted to believe him, but I'd heard those words countless times, usually moments before they were proved wrong.

He leaned away far enough that he could see my face. "Never."

I looked into his eyes, expecting to see the yellow fire. There was no wolf to be found. Just Mason's calm, blue eyes staring back at me. His lips weren't pinched and tight. No menacing ridge creased his brow. Just a soft furrow to punctuate his concern.

I nodded again, this time meaning it.

He pulled me back into his arms. "You don't have to do this alone."

I put my hands around him and squeezed. For the moment, I felt entirely safe.

His lips pressed against the top of my head. The stubble that had grown overnight prickled, even through my hair, beckoning me to touch it.

"You, Jane"—he laid a hand along my cheek—"you're the one I want. Ever since I caught you talking to that silly, neon fish."

"What about Jennica?"

"What about her?" he said. "You know, I'm new in this city too. When I saw you in the grocery store and mistook you for her, I thought, 'Here's someone I know. Why not try to reconnect?' Imagine my surprise when the temperamental, self-centered girl from high school turned out to be kind and funny and smart. But every time we got close, you gave me the cold shoulder.

"Then, Saturday, I came to see you, hoping we could work it out. I missed you. Suddenly, you were warm and affectionate. I guess I let my excitement cloud my judgment. But honestly, how many times can one set of twins hoodwink little old me? Clearly I didn't suspect more than once."

He sounded sincere, and his words made sense. Maybe if I had trusted him right from the first, we could have avoided this whole mess. I should have been honest from the beginning. But trust and honesty were not the protocols I had been raised with.

"Are you saying you want to start over?" I asked. A clean slate sounded nice. But risky. I stepped away. "Because what happens the next time Jennica shows up? How do I know I can trust you?" I paced the narrow width of the living room. "Not just with her but with everything. And how do you know you can trust me? I let you believe I was someone I'm not. What happens next time I do something stupid? Or make a mistake?" I'd felt so sure only moments ago, but now misty doubts leaked in, blurring the edges. "How do I know you're not a wolf in sheep's clothing?"

"You don't." He shook his head. "Then again, nothing ventured, nothing gained. It's a risk we both have to take. The truth is, we've only known each other for a few weeks. But there is something powerful between us. I know you feel it too."

I did feel it, though I dared not admit it because that would make it real. Reality had a way of disappointing.

"I don't want to start over," he went on. "I want to pick up right here, right now. I want to keep our dinner at Red Marlin and our long waits in the hospital. I want to keep you, now, with your flannel pajamas and tangled hair." He stepped close, resting his hands on my shoulders. "I know what I want, Jane. The question is, what do you want?"

The moment he touched me, I sensed it again. Just like that day in the hospital, after all the tests and stress with my mom. He'd steadied me and held me and let me cry. That was what I felt now—a kind of grounding. Like these past five years I'd been a tent flapping in the wind, struggling not to collapse. Until Mason had come along and staked me down.

I knew what I wanted. I wanted a gentle man. A sheep in sheep's clothing. But also someone strong and capable. I wanted to close my eyes, lean in, and press my lips into his thicket of whiskers.

Mason. I wanted him.

I looped my arms around his neck. "I want you to stop using so many clichés," I told him, offering up my heart on a platter. He was wearing off on me already.

With a satisfied smile on his face, he took me in his arms and kissed me.

OTHER BOOKS BY JULIE DAINES

A Blind Eye

Unraveled